Brigham's Ghost Brigade

The Case of the Deadly Counterfeiters

Brigham's Ghost Brigade

The Case of the Deadly Counterfeiters

Ron Carter

Harbour Books

Claremont, California

Published by:
Harbour Books
147 Armstrong
Claremont, CA 91711

Library of Congress Preassign:
96-075394

paperback ISBN: 0-964-3672-4-6

Book Development: Barbara Ciletti
Text design and production: Graphic Relations
Cover design & illustration: Greg Michaels
Color Separation: Capitol Engraving, Denver, CO
Printing: Publishers Press, Salt Lake City, Utah

10 9 8 7 6 5 4 3 2 1

Introduction

The history of the early Church is rich with thrilling adventures for all ages. The spread of the gospel from its modest beginnings in Palmyra, New York, westward to Iowa and Ohio, and Missouri, gave us many heroes and faith building stories.

Perhaps the most inspiring event was the westward migration across the trackless prairies to a great basin in the legendary Rocky Mountains - a basin where a salt inland sea was cradled in granite mountains that touched the sky. Wagons, handcarts, horseback, on foot, - they came to fulfill the the prophesy of Brigham Young, in that high and desolate valley. "We will make it blossom as the rose."

And they did. But not without constant vigilance, for there were always conspiring men who sought to discredit or bring down the Lord's chosen, if they could. Brigham Young, the Lion of the Lord, understood all too well that such men were drawn to the valley, and he kept a watchful eye for them, through a few chosen men he trusted with his life. Of these men, none stood closer to the Prophet than Orrin Porter Rockwell.

One scheme to bring down the Prophet was attempted by two men who counterfeited government quartermaster notes, used to pay the soldiers at Fort Floyd. The counterfeiters thought they could pass the notes and get rich, then blame the Prophet in a plan to have him imprisoned for the crime. The Prophet heard rumors of the plot, and eventually the two men were jailed.

I have loved such stories from those pioneer days. Then one day I wondered, what would have happened if Brigham Young had turned to some teenagers for help in solving some of the perplexing problems of his time?

What would become of a series of books in which our heroes were teenagers, - as in many true instances was the case? It was but a short step from the thought to the act, and the first of the Ghost Brigade series was born.

The counterfeiting plot against the Prophet is historically true, as was the fact that Porter Rockwell was involved in exposing it. But from there, well, Porter said it best himself. "You kids are out there in town right under their noses, doing all this, and no one has an idea. Like a bunch of ghosts. Brigham's Ghost Brigade." And if Porter was right, - if Seth, Libby, Hawk, Jacob and Abe were clever and crafty enough to solve the mysteries given them by the Prophet without being detected, who among us can say that what follows is not the truth?

Ron Carter

One

"YER TO COME WITH ME, lad." Seth Dunn's long, lean fifteen year old frame jerked erect in the milking shed and he spun, probing. A murky figure moved in the deep shadows of a corner and Seth dropped the milk bucket he had just cleaned, and snatched up a pitchfork.

"Get out here where I can see you, and you better say who you are, mister," Seth said, "or you'll have some trouble with this." He raised the fork, balanced, ready.

The figure stepped into the yellow circle of lanternlight and stood with feet apart, arms hanging loosely at his sides. He was average height, solid frame. A black, wide brimmed, low crowned hat sat squarely on his head, and his shoulder length hair caught the yellow lantern glow and framed his face, and his eyes glowed like embers. He wore a loose, black frock coat.

"No harm intended, lad. Yer to come with me."

"Not likely. Who are you? What do you want?"

"Name's Porter. Come along."

"Not 'til I know where, and why. You look to me like one of those tinhorn gamblers from Camp Floyd."

"Humph," the man grunted. "Well, I been called worse. I give you my word, it's important. No harm will come to you as long as you're with me."

"Where?"

"To the City Creek canal. A man wants to talk to you."

"What man?"

"He'll tell you when you get there. If yer comin', come. If not, say so and I'll tell him."

"You armed?"

A crooked smile broke through the full beard. "Two pistols and a sawed off shotgun and a Bowie knife. If I'da been here to do you harm you'da been dead when you walked in the door. You comin' or not? I'm tired of jawin'."

Seth's curiosity was piqued; he could not resist. "You lead out. I got this fork right behind you."

The man shook his head. "Suit yerself."

Without another word he turned and stalked out of the milking shed into the night and headed north towards the large canal that diverted water south from City Creek, down past the Liberty Ward building and Liberty Park, to irrigate the south reaches of Salt Lake City. Seth followed through the corral connected to the barn where the old family Jersey cow, Mossie, worked patiently on her cud. They crossed second east, where fine dust lay warm in the soft, late May moonlight.

Seth glanced west towards downtown Salt Lake City where lights glittered from a few shops and the Salt Lake Theatre, and he could see the faint outline of the walls of the Temple, now nearly to the second floor. The skeletal bones of the round dome of the tabernacle stood in stark relief against the velvet sky, waiting for the roof to cover them.

Seth Edward Dunn stood six feet tall and was just

coming into a full man's frame. His dark hair was stubborn, and his heavy brow made his dark eyes look slightly cavernous. His nose was prominent, his jaw square, and all together, he was a striking young man. He was also the Thinker for the Liberty Stake in Salt Lake City, Desert Territory. If you needed something thought about, or planned, or analyzed, eventually you got to young Seth Dunn. His curiosity was legendary, and had gotten him into so many predicaments that his mother often declared Seth might survive his growing up years, but she was sure she would not.

Seth licked dry lips and walked cautiously, set, wary, ready to move any direction, or run at the first sign of an ambush. His guide walked in the deep shadows of the trees that lined second east, and slowed as he came to the huge irrigation ditch. He walked into a small cluster of aspens and Seth stopped five feet from him, waiting.

A figure emerged seemingly from nowhere, and even in the filigree of light and dark sifting through the trees, Seth saw the power in the stride and felt it in the square, blocky build of the man.

"Brother Dunn, I presume?"

The man walked directly to Seth and extended his hand, and for an instant Seth froze. The voice! He knew the voice! He had heard it raised like thunder in the Liberty Ward building, and in the Bowery, and in the yet unfinished tabernacle! That voice had testified to the divine mission of Joseph Smith, and like the roar of a lion it had testified that Jesus Christ is the Son of God, and it is He, Jesus Christ, who heads this Church!

Brigham Young! Moonlight shined off the flat planes of the square face and the bulldog set of the jaw, and the prominent nose.

Seth swallowed and held the fork in his hands, forgotten.

"Brother Dunn?," the voice asked again.

Seth shook himself. "Yes sir. Are you . . ."

"Yes I am."

"President Young? The Prophet?"

"I'm Brigham Young."

Seth shifted the fork and thrust out his hand. "I'm pleased to meet you, sir," and they shook hands, and Seth felt the raw power in the grip of the thick hand.

"I'm pleased to meet you, too. Have a minute we could talk?"

Seth looked back down Second East towards his home. "I think so. Chores are done."

His guide faded into the trees and was instantly invisible, but he was still there.

"You want to lean that fork against a tree?"

Seth stammered, "Yes sir. No offense meant."

"None taken." President Young locked his hands behind his back and paced two or three paces back and forth while he talked.

"Bishop Lundgren tells me you're a good, steady, reliable young man with friends who are the same. I think I need you and your friends. Rumor has it there are some bad men who are conspiring to slander me and destroy the church. I also know that there are a lot of counterfeit quartermaster notes being spread around the valley, as though they came from the paymaster at Camp Floyd. You know about Camp Floyd?"

"Yes sir. Down west of Utah Lake. And I know about Fairfield. Frog Town. Pretty bad, so I hear."

"You heard right, son. An abomination. But back to the problem, it looks like whoever is circulating those counterfeit notes intends to accuse me of it, and claim I did it to get the Army down at Camp Floyd in trouble. They want me arrested and put on trial and sent to a federal prison, hoping the church will crumble while I'm gone."

Seth swallowed hard. "Someone's going to arrest you?"

Brigham Young straightened and locked Seth with a direct stare. "Never doubt it, son, there are enemies of the Lord that would do it in an instant if they could. They killed Joseph, and they drove us two thousand miles."

"What can I do, sir?"

"I sent some brethren to find out what they could, but wherever they go, whoever they ask, they get no answers at all, partly because people don't know, and partly because people are afraid to take sides against bad men who might harm them if they found out who told."

Brigham paused and Seth stared hard at him for a moment in deep thought.

"So," Brigham continued, "it appears I've sent out the wrong people. I think a good, steady, wide awake young man, with a few friends he can trust, might be able to find out what the Elders can not."

Seth gulped. "You want me to find out about this counterfeiting thing?"

Brigham young stopped pacing and squared himself with Seth. "Exactly."

"How do I do that, sir?"

"I'll leave that to you. If you're the young man Bishop Lundgren says you are, you and your friends will find a way. There are just a few principles you must abide."

"What are they?"

"Foremost, I want no violence, no one hurt or killed. Clear?"

"Clear."

"No one must know what you're about except the guide who brought you here."

"Okay."

"If anyone finds out, I will have to remain silent. I can not jeopardize either of us by saying I was using you. I will not lie about it, I will simply remain silent. I cannot step up and defend you if you're discovered.

Do you understand?"

"I understand."

"Do not come directly to me. If you need me, tell the man who brought you here. He'll take care of it."

"When should all this begin?"

"Now. Tonight."

Seth's eyes bulged. "Tonight? I'm supposed to start tonight?"

Brigham nodded his head.

"How about my mother? Can she know?"

"No."

"I'm going to have to be gone from home a lot. I got chores. How do I handle that?"

"I leave that to you."

Seth shrugged and exhaled heavily. "This sounds pretty wild."

"It could be. My deepest concern is for your safety. Evil men will do anything to stop you, maybe even kidnap you or kill you. Do you understand?"

"Yes."

"All right. If you think you can help without being caught or hurt, I would like you to try. But you must promise you will cease the moment you sense real danger to you or your friends, and you will tell the guide who brought you here. Agreed?"

Seth turned and widened his eyes in the gloom, but could barely make out the form of the silent guide in the trees, standing vigil while the two talked.

"Agreed."

"You want to give it a try?"

"Yes. I'll try."

"Thank you. Your Bishop said you would."

"Does he know about this?"

"No. He only knows I asked him if he knew a strong, steady young man with good friends for a difficult assignment."

"Okay." Brigham Young stretched out his hand.

"Thank you, Brother Dunn. God bless you. I won't forget this."

Seth picked up his pitchfork. "One more thing. Who is the guide?"

Brigham softly whistled the call of a mourning dove and the guide materialized from the trees.

"Brother Dunn, I would like you to meet Orrin Porter Rockwell."

Seth gasped and stood rooted to the ground while the fork dropped from his hand unnoticed.

This man had been called everything! The Destroying Angel. Murderer. Villain. Assassin. Danite. Bodyguard of two prophets. Inseparable friend, loved by Joseph Smith. Close, beloved friend of Brigham Young. Gunfighter. Knife fighter. Indian fighter. Tracker. Scourge of all evil men. Indestructible. Chosen of the Lord to help lead the saints west, their scout, their guardian, their angel in the wilderness.

Seth could not force a word; he could only raise his hand and point.

"Yes, that's him." Seth saw Brigham's shoulders shake in silent mirth.

A chuckle rolled from deep in Rockwell's chest. "In the flesh, lad."

Porter turned to Brigham. "I think you picked the right man. When I come out of the shadows in that milkin' shed, fer a minit I figgered he meant to stick me with that fork. Pecky lad."

Seth stammered, "I . . you got to excuse that . . I didn't know."

"'Course you didn't. I'da done the same."

Brigham looked at Porter. "You understand he'll report to you, not me?"

"Old wheat in the mill," Porter replied, still smiling.

Seth looked at Brigham for a translation.

"That's Porter's way of saying everything will be all right."

"Old Wheat in the mill?"

"Or just 'wheat'. Yes."

"How do I contact Mr. Porter?"

Porter said, "Don't call me mister; just Porter. Maybe you won't see me, but I'll usually be near by, or down in my room at the back of the Lion House. Whistle like a mourning dove. If that don't work, leave word at the Hotel Utah downtown. I'll find you."

Brigham interrupted. "Brother Dunn, you better go on back home before you're missed. Check in with Porter at least every second day. You have my blessing, son."

"Thank you, sir," Seth said.

He took his fork and moved silently out of the small clump of trees, back down second east, but instead of heading straight to the milk shed behind his home, he cut across the vacant lot behind Hossfelder's place, vaulted the fence into the back yard of Hosea Pierce, and stopped with the fork still in his hands. He picked up a small clod and lobbed it clinking against the glass in a second floor bedroom window.

The window jerked open and the upper half of a tow headed fourteen year old boy leaned out. "Hey, who's down there?," he called. "What's going on?"

"Shush," Seth hissed, "it's me. Someone'll hear!"

"Why didn't you say so," the hoarse whisper replied. The boy turned away and Seth heard him say, "No, mama it's just me. There was something in the back yard but it's gone. I'm going to bed." A door closed, and the bedroom lamp went out and the window went black.

Two minutes later a dark form slipped over the window sill, hung briefly, and dropped to the ground.

Jacob Jeremy Pierce, fourteen, slender, not as tall as Seth, blue eyed, tow headed, handsome even in his growing years, quickly trotted to Seth.

At age twelve Jacob Pierce had used his father's muzzle loading Hawken rifle at the July 24th celebration for the shooting contest. Against all comers - mountain men, gunmen, law men, outlaws, —young Jacob's fifty caliber ball had cut the center out of the bullseye ten times in succession to win the coveted prize, a new Henry .44-40 repeater rifle, and he cut ten more targets to win a case of ammunition. In the following two years Jacob had become one of the finest riflemen in the territory. He fed the families of three widows through the winter with his rifle, and not once had he wasted meat. Each deer or elk he brought back from the east Wasatch mountains had but one bullet hole - through the head, quick and merciful.

"What's going on?," Jacob whispered.

"You aren't going to believe this," Seth said, and Jacob heard the urgency in his voice.

Five minutes later Jacob clacked his gaping mouth shut, then spoke. "Brigham Young? Orrin Porter Rockwell? Seth, did Mossie kick you in the head?"

Seth looked pained. "No, Mossie didn't kick me in the head. Get serious, Jacob. I just got back from the meeting. We got to get the others and get to work. You tell Libby and Hawk. I'll tell Abe. We'll meet at five o'clock in the morning, over by the well house behind the Ward building."

"No, you tell Libby. She's in love with you, not me. I'll get Abe and Hawk."

"Aw, come on, cut out that love stuff. Libby says she intends marrying you after your mission, not me. Get her and Hawk. Okay?"

"She didn't say no such thing."

"Did too. Get moving."

"When?"

"When what?"

"When did she say something that stupid?"

"After sacrament meeting last Sunday evening, out by the horses and buggies."

"I didn't hear it."

"Well, she said it. She's staked her claim on you."

"Horsefeathers."

"Get moving."

Jacob moved out like a shadow and disappeared around the corner of the house, ran two blocks south and one east, and came up behind the big brick house that dominated the corner of fourth south and third east. He silently vaulted the back fence, waited until his breathing slowed, then swung lightly up into a big cottonwood tree that stood on one side of the back yard. In a moment he was sitting on a huge branch near a second story window. He leaned forward and tapped lightly, three times.

A minute later the window opened one inch.

"Who's there?," came the whisper.

"Me. Jacob."

"Jacob who?"

"Goldarn it Libby," Jacob growled, "what do you mean, Jacob who? You know dang well Jacob who. What other Jacob knows how to get to this window, Stupid."

The window opened wider and a head thrust out, with one great braid hanging over a shoulder. Even in the shadows of the gables of the great house, Jacob could see her heart shaped face with the freckled, turned up nose and the blue eyes and the generous mouth, and he knew that one day she would be a beauty.

Libby Taylor knew just about everything about almost everybody in Salt Lake Valley, and once she set her mind to it could manipulate more people to do what she wanted than any other female in town, and age was no barrier. Libby had decided Liberty Park needed a cement lined wading pool, and when she finished, her father, the Mayor, had no inkling the whole idea was not his own. The city mothers had showered him with thanks when they sat beneath the great cottonwoods in the August heat and watched their toddlers splashing in the cool waters of the shallow pool. Mayor Taylor congratulated himself on his stroke of genius, while Libby smiled.

"Not stupid," she exclaimed, "just cautious. A girl's got

to protect herself."
Jacob winced. "At thirteen? From what?"
"Boys."
"Boys doing what?"
Libby Taylor puckered her forehead and considered. "I don't know. Mama hasn't told me that part yet. And I'm not thirteen. I'm fourteen next week."
"Okay, you're fourteen. Seth says we got to meet at the Ward well house at five o'clock in the morning. I think Mossie kicked him in the head. Be there."
"Meet about what? Is he trying to get us to plant widow Pickard's garden again? It's already done and besides he's too late because it's nearly June."
"No, nothing like that."
"Then what. I'm not coming if you don't tell."
Jacob shook his head. "If that's not just like a woman. Okay, I'll tell you. Brigham Young wants him to help catch a bunch of criminals to save the church and Seth needs us to help and we report to Orrin Porter Rockwell and we got to keep this secret. Does that satisfy you?"
"You're right."
Jacob nearly fell out of the tree. Libby usually dangled people, left them on tender hooks. She never came out with such a bold, final statement as "You're right."
"Right about what," he blurted.
"Mossie kicked him in the head."
"I mighta known. Seth says five o'clock. He's got to make plans. Be there."
The window closed and Jacob was out of the tree in thirty seconds, running north at a steady pace to temple square. He slipped past the great piles of dirt removed for the temple foundations, past granite blocks weighing ten tons, through the Bowery, to a small shed on the southwest corner and rapped on the door. It opened and two steady eyes peered at him from an Indian face.
"Seth wants us at the Liberty Ward well house at five

o'clock in the morning. Be there."

Hawk, a Ute Indian boy of unknown age, found nearly dead on temple square in a January blizzard years ago, nursed back to health and adopted and mothered and fathered and watched over by half of the saints in Salt Lake City, had been given a shed on the southwest corner of temple square to call his own. He preferred to have his own place.

Someone in his Indian childhood had taught Hawk to track like a master. It was Hawk who tracked the lost Sorensen girl for two days when she wandered from the picnic site up Emigration canyon, and found the six year old wedged beneath a great windfall cedar. It was Hawk who had been called out by the Elders to track a renegade killer for four days, and Hawk ran him to ground in a rocky canyon south of Brigham City. His reputation had spread. Hawk, the Indian boy from Salt Lake City, could track a shadow over rocks. And Hawk could vanish like magic, when it was needed.

Hawk looked steadily at Jacob and nodded once. He would be there.

Down south of Liberty Park, Seth trotted to the light in the barn of the Rawlins place, and peered through the crack in the door. Inside, Abraham Rawlins, age fifteen, small, slight, wiry, quick in his movements, held the lead rope of a halter while he carefully, lovingly worked a curry brush over the withers and down the shoulders and legs of a beautiful, nine year old, dapple gray, full blood Arabian mare. His father, Josephus Rawlins, had brought the mare from Virginia, guarding and protecting it with his very life every mile of the way, so he would have the foundation of a great herd of blooded Arabians when they arrived in the valley.

Abe had fallen in love with the mare, named her Star, trained, taught, rode, curried, and cared for her, and it was Abe who could mount her from any side without saddle or bridle, grab a handfull of mane and ride her like the wind, as though the two were one. The mare loved Abe, trusted him, would run to his whistle, kneel, and nod to him, and no one questioned she would run her heart out for him if he asked her to do it. Word spread. You got a horse needs trained, get the Rawlins kid. He talks to horses.

Seth walked in and Abe turned.

"Seth! You're out late," he said.

"You aren't going to believe this."

Five minutes later Abe shook himself. "You're right. I don't believe it."

"Be at the well house at five o'clock in the morning. We've got to plan."

Two

SETH RAN A BRUSH through his intractable hair, slipped into his pants and shirt and grabbed his high topped shoes and his socks and crept downstairs, out through the kitchen door, onto the back porch. He sat to tie his shoes, and trotted past the root cellar just as Old Boxer, the family rooster, pounded the air with stubby wings and announced from the top of the henhouse that a bright new day was in the making.

The light clouds above the mountains were shot with streaks of pinks and reds as Seth scooped grain from the feed bin and tossed it through the wire into the chicken yard and headed south at a run. Five minutes later he slowed and stopped at the low, unpainted, weather worn well house behind the Liberty Ward building where Abe, Hawk and Jacob sat waiting.

"Where's Libby?," he asked.

"I told her to be here," Jacob said defensively.

"We'll have to start without her," Seth replied.

"Hold it," Abe interjected, "here she comes."

Libby walked sedately past the corner of the Ward building and they waited while she continued over to stand at the corner of well house.

"Just like a woman, - made us all wait," muttered Jacob.

Libby folded her arms and looked down her nose at them, seated on the ground. "What's all this about, Seth Dunn," she demanded.

"Just settle down and listen," he said.

Ten minutes later he finished. "And that's the gospel truth of it."

All eyes were wide in disbelief, all mouths hung open in stunned surprise.

"US?," Abe said. "Catch counterfeiters?"

Seth nodded. "Us."

Jacob ballooned his cheeks as he exhaled held breath. "Okay, what's the plan?," he said to Seth. "You're the thinking department."

Seth pursed his mouth and pulled his upper lip, as he always did when wondrous and immense things were shaping in his mind.

"I think we're going into the newspaper business."

Libby's head jerked forward. "Newspaper business? To find counterfeiters?"

"Yes. Think about it," Seth said, and he began to pace as the words spilled out. "To make counterfeit bills they've got to have ink, and paper, and some kind of printing press. Newspapers and book publishers use all those things, and Brother Dudley runs the only newspaper and print shop in town. And newspaper people can go anywhere and ask anybody anything."

"So Brother Dudley is the counterfeiter? HAH!", exclaimed Jacob.

"No of course not. Come on, get serious. But one thing is sure. Either the counterfeiters used Dudley's stuff, or they got their own. If they got their own, they shipped it in somehow, and if they did that, it came in through either the freight office or the Bishop's storehouse because they're the only freight depots in town and they should have records."

"What if they snuck it in on a wagon one dark night and hid it somewhere?," Jacob asked.

"They could have," Seth said, "but if they did, they had to set it up in some place big enough to print and trim, and if they work at night they'll need light."

"So," Libby said, "we're looking for some place that is big enough to print money and has light at night? Like the Salt Lake Theatre or the Ward house, or the Bowery, or Hotel, or the temple, or forty other places in town."

"Come on, Libby," Seth retorted. "After it's printed, they've got to have some system to spread it around town, and down at Camp Floyd, and in Frog Town."

"Frog Town?" Abe exclaimed. "Man, if any of us go down there, we're taking Jacob and his rifle."

Seth resumed pacing. "Now let's put it all together. First we need to persuade Brother Dudley to let us print a monthly Junior Editorial or something, for his Desert Examiner. Libby, you can handle that."

Libby's eyes opened wide in question but she said nothing.

Seth pulled his upper lip for a moment. "Once he says yes, then we're in the newspaper business, and we can start asking questions all over town about all kinds of stuff."

He stopped pacing and turned to Abe. "Then we got to get somebody working inside Brother Dudley's shop to learn about printing. Abe, you're quick with your hands. Think you could be a printer's apprentice?"

"Me? I got chores. I got to take care of Star and the horses."

"Do your chores early in the morning. You can spend half a day with Brother Dudley once in a while."

Seth continued pacing back and forth in the dust.

"Then we got to ask the freighters and the freight depot about the cost of shipping in a printing press, and if they've freighted in anything like that lately. I'll do that."

He turned to Hawk, who sat silent, attentive. "Then we got to have someone who's located where they can hear things from all over town. Hawk, that's you. Everybody in the valley works on the temple at one time or another, and you're right there. Just be around, listening. Sooner or later someone's going to say or do something. Understand?"

Hawk bobbed his head and remained silent.

"Jacob, you're about to become our head newspaper reporter. Get a notebook and pencil, and put a badge on and start asking around. Do articles on everything you can think of. Visit everybody. Ask every question you can think of, but be careful not to tip them off to what we're doing. Okay?"

"Wait a minute!," Jacob exclaimed. "I hate being nosy. I keep my nose in my own business, mainly."

"I said you're our head reporter, not our only reporter. We're all going to be reporters."

He turned to Libby. "And you're going to be the one who gets into the best gossip pipeline in the valley."

Libby's eyes opened wide. "I am? What?"

"The Relief Society. You're a natural. There's nothing happens this side of Winter Quarters that the Relief Society doesn't know about ten minutes later."

Libby's mouth became a straight line and her eyes flashed. "So you think the Relief Society is for gossip?"

Seth looked exasperated. "Of course not! The Church couldn't survive without the sisters. Will you do it?"

Libby cleared her throat. "I'll think about it."

"Good. Okay. That's it. Anybody got any better ideas?"

No one spoke.

"About your parents, tell them this is another one of

our projects, - going into the newspaper business for the summer. Tell them we should make a little money and get a lot of good experience and mostly that it will keep us out of trouble 'til school starts in the fall. That should persuade 'em. Now, scatter and get busy. We'll meet back here at five in the morning. Libby, good luck with old Dudley. If you don't persuade him, this whole thing comes apart."

At eleven o'clock Libby changed from her work clothes to a street dress, brushed back a lock of errant hair, stood erect in front of the mirror in her room and turned slightly. She watched herself while she changed her expression, first to serious, then curious, then enthralled, then wide eyed innocence, then utterly charming. She giggled at herself. Satisfied she had it all working, she walked sedately out the door for the street.

"Eight rods," Brigham had declared, and eight rods they were. One hundred thirty two feet, curb to curb. Wide enough to turn a six-up team of horses hooked to a freight wagon or a stagecoach, completely around. No other town on the continent had streets as wide as those of Salt Lake City, territory of Deseret.

Libby crossed the expanse of second east and headed north. Ten minutes later she walked through the door on South Temple with the sign above it, DESERET EXAMINER, Ebenezer Dudley, Prop.

Short and round and balding, old Brother Dudley glanced up.

"Mornin', Libby. Looking nice. What can I do for you?" He kept working with a wooden mallet and small lead blocks with letters on them. Black arm garters held up the ink stained sleeves of his white shirt, and a green visor shaded his eyes.

"I just came by to ask about . . ." She stopped. "My, that looks interesting. What are you doing, if I may ask?" She put on her curious look. Dudley looked at her.

"Setting print." Her big blue eyes widened. "With a hammer?"

"No," Dudley smiled, "just a wooden mallet. The letters are made of soft lead, so we use a wooden mallet that won't hurt them."

"How utterly thrilling! Do you mind if I just watch or a minute?"

Dudley's hands stopped for a moment while he looked at her, trying to understand what could be utterly thrilling about pounding lead letters with a wooden mallet. "No, not at all."

He worked on for a minute while Libby put on her enchanted look and stood stone still, gazing.

"My," she exclaimed, "wouldn't it be rewarding to be able to do that. Do you put all those letters together for each edition of your newspaper?"

"Every one of them."

"I just can't imagine . . ." She let her voice trail off while she put on her wondrous expression.

"Oh, it's nothing," Dudley said, and continued picking letters from the large, partitioned tray, and tapping them into place.

He glanced at her again. "Is that what brought you here? You wanted to see type setting?"

Libby shook herself as though lost in a trance. "Oh. No. Goodness no, but that's just so . . . interesting . . I came over to ask if you were going to include an article about the new project."

Dudley stopped. "What project?"

"The one . . . You haven't heard?" She put on her startled look.

His reporter's instincts aroused, Dudley put down his mallet and began wiping his hands with a badly ink stained towel. "I won't know 'til you tell which project you're talking about."

"The summer youth project. About starting youth

patrols in the evening to watch the city streets. There's some concern about the soldiers from Johnston's army down at camp Floyd, and all the new people arriving, making the streets unsafe after dark. Maybe the youth could set up evening patrols to watch."

Dudley fixed her with a cocked eye. "Seth been at it again?"

"Seth? Oh, no. The young ladies, mostly. It's us that are fearful."

Dudley arched his eyebrows in surprise. "Say, you might have something there. Who could I ask about all this?"

"Well, I don't know exactly, but if you want me to I'll try to find out."

"Yeah, that would be good. Make it soon. I go to press in a few days."

"Why I'd be delighted." She put on her charming look. "Thank you. My, I just can't believe how interesting this must all be."

Dudley glanced around at the friendly clutter of his office. "It has its rewards."

"I'll be back after I've learned who you should talk to."

For two hours Libby browsed through the Bishop's Storehouse, and Zion's Cooperative Mercantile Institution, looking at all the latest fashions in ladies wear and hats. Then she walked back towards Dudley's office, and ran the last two blocks, and burst through the door, flushed, breathless. Dudley spun in surprise to face her.

"Oh, Mr. Dudley," she panted. "The most wonderful idea."

She pressed her hand against her throat while she battled to slow her labored breathing.

"The youth," she began, and then stopped while she fought for more breath.

"Yes," he said, leaning slightly forward onto the counter. "Go on. The youth what?"

"Would you . . let us . . ," she paused again to gasp for breath.

"Libby, slow down. Would I let you what?"

"We've been talking. We would just love to write up a little article for your newspaper. By the youth. Just this once. We want to make a public proposal that we be allowed to organize and set up our own evening patrols for the summer."

"You kids want to write an editorial?"

"Yes. We'll do it any way you say. Just this once."

"Who you been talking to?"

"Janie and Jessica and Sarah, and Seth, and . . just lots of us."

She put on her pleading look, the one that would wrench the heart out of a stone statue.

"Well, I'll have to think about it. Will Seth help organize it? That kid's got the knack."

"Yes. Oh yes, Seth will take charge."

Dudley tipped his head back and scratched beneath his chin. "Well, I don't know . . ."

"Oh, Mr. Dudley, please please please."

He lowered his head and his face puckered. "Just this once?"

"Well, to start."

"Now wait a minute," Dudley said, "what do you mean, to start."

Libby straightened and put on her business look. "Mr. Dudley, let me ask you one question. How would you like to increase your newspaper business, maybe double?"

"How?"

"Us kids."

His eyebrows arched. "Are you suggesting . . ."

Libby stood silent and watched while his mind raced.

"You mean," Dudley said, "start a kids editorial section in the newspaper? Every edition?"

"Oh, how wonderful," Libby bubbled. "Besides our youth patrols, the first edition could be a survey of businesses in town to see how fast the valley is growing. You could mention a lot of businesses by name, and the owners, and they'd get free publicity that way, and it would sell millions of papers for you."

He turned and started to pace. "Might not be a bad idea. Might be pretty good. Yeah. Might be pretty good."

"How would you circulate it," Libby challenged.

He jabbed a finger in the air as though he had just received a revelation. "Can you kids handle that, too?"

"Oh, how original! Why, you're a genius. Of course. The kids could set up routes in town and sell newspapers. Maybe they could make a penny or two off what they sell."

"By Jove, it might just work," Dudley said.

Libby looked worshipful. "I can't believe how you thought all this up so quickly," she said. "Can we do it? Can we try it just this once and see if it will work, and if it does, maybe we can do it off and on this summer?"

"Tell you what. You work up this first editorial. If it's good, we'll give it a try."

"Oh Mr. Dudley," she said, and put on her devastating look. "You're wonderful! I'll go tell the others and Seth will get busy."

She dashed out the door, down to Main, and slowed to a walk, and looked back to be sure Brother Dudley was not watching.

She looked self satisfied, and said, "That's that," under her breath, and continued south on Main towards City Hall. Approaching, she watched the workers patiently walking on the scaffolding to set the newly cut stones as the building grew steadily upward. She picked her way through the construction, to the front door, and down the hall to the big door marked "MAYOR BENJAMIN TAYLOR", and walked in.

"'Morning, Libby," Ruth Livingston, the secretary,

said. Ruth was tall and officious and very protective of the mayor.

"Come to see your father?"

"Yes. Is he in?"

"He's in a meeting."

"Will it last long?"

"Probably. He said . . ."

The door into his private office rattled and opened, and a man dressed in work clothes, with a lot of rolled up papers, walked out, followed by her father.

"Okay," the man said, "we'll do it just like on the plans. Just trying to save some time and money."

Benjamin Taylor was average height, well built, becoming a little pudgy in the middle, usually gentle, sometimes strict when the occasion demanded, and loved by most of the people in the valley.

"Follow the plans. Keeps us both out of trouble with the city council."

The man strode briskly from the room and Benjamin Taylor noticed his daughter.

"Libby! What brings you here?," he asked.

"I thought you'd like to hear some good news."

"About what?"

"Your idea."

His forehead wrinkled. "What idea?"

"The one we discussed three weeks ago."

He shook his head. "Come on in. I seem to have forgotten."

Ruth watched Libby follow her father into his office and close the door before she mumbled, "His idea - nonsense. She's at it again."

"What idea did we discuss?"

"About the evening patrols. You remember."

"Well, vaguely, something . . what was it?"

"We're going to organize evening patrols among the young people, by Wards, with three or four in each group, and a leader. They'll patrol the streets against undesireables from Camp Floyd, or the strangers moving to town."

Benjamin shook his head. "Don't remember a thing."

"Oh daddy, of course you do," she said and looked demure. "Brother Dudley thought your idea was wonderful. He's going to run a special editorial on it."

Benjamin's eyebrows arched in surprise. "He is? All the voters will see it? Tell me about it."

"Well, first, do you approve of it? Could he put that in his editorial?"

"Sounds like a good idea. Why not? Give me the details."

* * *

Hawk stacked the last of the split kindling against the back wall of Sister Galley's log cabin just as the back door opened and Ellen Galley hobbled out on her cane.

"Hawk, you come on in here and eat," she said brusquely. "Land, the way you been workin' you should eat a pile."

He followed her into the kitchen and sat down to turnip greens and baked chicken and mashed potatoes and berry pie. He ate silently while Ellen watched with a satisfied eye.

"Thank you, ma'am," he said as he stood and wiped on a napkin.

"Thanks to you, young man. Same time next week?"

Hawk nodded.

"Now you come visit me over the weekend. Things get lonely with Caleb gone. You hear me?"

"I will."

Hawk set out at his steady trot, up west seventh to south temple, then east to temple square, back to his shed. He changed from moccasins to work shoes and walked back out, towards the crew handling stone for the temple.

"This Temple to the Lord will be built only with the finest stone we can find," Brigham had said, and the best stone was granite from twenty miles up Big Cottonwood Canyon, southeast of Sale Lake City. Willing hands cut it in five and ten ton blocks, skidded them down to sleds, and thick necked oxen leaned into heavy oaken yokes to drag the sleds down the canyon, to temple square. It had gone on for twelve years and would go on for twenty eight more before the temple was pronounced completed.

Hawk picked up a shovel to throw rock shards into a pile. Clearing rock shards from the area where the stonecuters chiseled at granite blocks, never stopped.

A broad shouldered brother swung a sledge. "Heard about Camp Floyd," he asked his partner.

"Nope."

"Buchanan might call the army back."

Talk went on.

A pair of teamsters passed, one with a twenty-foot bullwhip wrapped about his shoulder.

"Sixty mules. Yessir, they stole sixty of 'em. Don't know how we're goin' to get 'em back. Maybe Rockwell can do it."

The teamsters passed.

"Where's the Bishop's storehouse?"

Hawk turned to see who did not know where to find the Bishop's storehouse. Everyone in the valley knew where it was. Tithing was paid there, usually in wheat or corn, or chickens or eggs, or potatoes or meat, or leather work, or anything of value. Needy came there to work, to earn their bread honorably. All paths in Salt Lake Valley eventually led to the Bishop's storehouse. Who did not know where it was?

Brother Yerrington pulled off his battered felt hat and wiped his sweaty forehead and faced two men. One was burly, thick shouldered and thick necked, and wore dirty corduroy pants and an army hat. The other was taller, more slender, with a full, scraggly beard, and a nose too red from drink.

"New in town?"

"Yeah. Where's the storehouse?"

"Which ward you in?"

"We don't know nothin' about no ward," growled the burly one, "we was told to find the Bishop's Storehouse."

"Need work?"

"No."

"Storehouse's right over there on first north and first east. The Bishop there'll explain how it works."

The men turned to leave.

"What's yer names," Yerrington called after them.

They ignored him and kept walking away. Brother Yerrington shook his head.

Hawk waited until Brother Yerrington returned to cutting a massive granite stone with his two pound hammer and chisel before he walked to where the two men had stood. He hunkered down and closely studied their footprints. Size, depth, hob nail imprints, weight on the inside or outside, heels or soles worn, does either one limp, is one leg short, - Hawk missed nothing. He might forget a name or a face, but in his life, he had never forgotten the print of a man or an animal. From a few good prints, Hawk could tell nearly anything anyone wanted to know about either one.

* * *

"Why Libby," crowed Hilda Gunderson, "how nice to have you visit us here in Relief Society."

"I hope you don't mind," Libby said coyly. "I just wanted to make some notes about what Relief Society is really like."

"Wonderful. We're about to begin. I'll announce you as a visitor. Why don't you just sit right here in front."

"Thank you."

Sister Gunderson turned to walk to the podium in the large, square room, filled with Sisters, and then she hesitated and turned back, puzzled.

"Take notes? What on earth for?"

"The newspaper editorial."

"How interesting. What editorial?"

"The one the youth are writing."

"The youth? What youth?"

Pearl Alexander nudged Hilda. "The sisters are waiting. Time to begin."

"In a moment," Hilda said, and continued. "Tell me more. What about the youth and the newspaper?"

"Oh that's not all! The Mayor approved a new evening patrol for the youth, and a survey of businesses in the valley, and so many things."

Hilda's eyes grew wide. "Your father approved what? Mercy, why haven't I heard about all this?"

Hilda Gunderson was affronted! When she was called to be Relief Society President, it became her sacred right to be informed of every tidbit, every morsel of news, no matter how trivial or insignificant, before anyone else. To have this stripling child know more than she did of the goings on in the valley was very close to sheer apostasy! That she would fix immediately.

"Why," said Libby, and looked innocent, "didn't you know? Everybody's been talking about it."

Hilda turned on her heel. "Pearl, you start this meeting. Sing Come Come Ye Saints, O My Father, We Thank Thee O God For A Prophet, - go through the entire song book if you have to, until I come back."

She spun back to Libby. "Now, young lady, you come with me. We'll get to the bottom of this!"

She marched out of the room with Libby following her adroitly, innocently.

Twenty minutes later Hilda marched back in, Libby following, still adroit and innocent.

Sister Gretta Schwartz heaved a great sigh of relief and

dropped her baton to stop the singing on the ninth verse of A Poor Wayfaring Man of Grief.

Hilda Gunderson's eyes were alive, sparkling with anticipation at the plums she was about to drop on the sisters.

"Sisters," she said, smiling grandly, "I have been authorized to bring to you two announcements that will change the history of this valley forever. They concern our youth. After months of prayer and work, we finally have approval of a proposal to save them from the evils forced upon us by the sinful soldiers from Camp Floyd, and the influence of evil drink and loose morals. We are all going to give our best support to this wonderful program. Our youth are going to organize into patrols to watch our streets in the evenings!"

"OOhhhh," and "aahhhh" drowned her out.

"And," she continued, "the youth are going to learn journalism under the kindly eye of Brother Dudley. They start a survey of businesses in the valley at once, for an editorial. Now, here are the details."

Every sister leaned forward and held their breath, lest they miss a single word.

Three

"LIBBY," SETH SAID, "YOU report first." Dark clouds sat heavy on the tops of the Wasatch mountains to the east. There was no morning sun; nothing stirred in the breathless hush of dead air.

Libby reported, and ended with, "So we are now in the newspaper business, and, we are supposed to organize youth patrols for the evening. We can do it by Wards. That way we will have the whole town covered, and know everything about who comes and goes at night."

"Terrific," grinned a jubilant Seth. "Where did you get the night patrol idea?"

Libby looked coy. "Why, I thought women are good for nothing more than gossip."

"Aw come on, Libby. You know better than that. The youth patrol thing is great. We'll start on that Sunday. We'll each visit two wards and in a couple weeks we'll have it all set up. They'll report anything suspicious to us, and to the High Council. And we can use the same organization to deliver the papers. Five papers sold, one penny earned. Every kid in the valley can earn a few dollars before school starts. Great idea."

Seth looked at Hawk. "Anything at temple square?"

Hawk spoke quietly, without emotion. "Don't know. Two men, looked bad, asked about the Bishop's storehouse. They were probably soldiers at one time, but not any more. They gave no names."

"Did they do something suspicious?"

"Not suspicious, but I think they would steal if they got the chance, or cheat with counterfeit money."

"What did they look like?"

"One was thick, heavy, the other taller and skinnier, and had a big red nose from too much whiskey."

"Okay," Seth said, "I'll check at the storehouse. Maybe Bishop Glade saw them."

He turned to Abe. "Go tell Brother Dudley you'd like to learn to set type and be his handyman, for free, some mornings. Ask questions about ink and paper. I'll head for the Storehouse and freight offices."

He said to Jacob, "Go with Abe and get Brother Dudley to let you be his chief reporter. Go see Brother Zollinger at ZCMI and ask about business. Find out if he's taken any counterfeit bills, but do it so he doesn't know why you asked. Act shocked if he has, and ask to see one so you'll see what colors are on it."

He faced Hawk again. "Go back to temple square and keep your eyes and ears open. You did good yesterday."

"Libby, follow up with some sisters. Youth patrols! You're a genius! Okay, scatter, and we'll meet back here at five in the morning."

They all glanced east at the billowing gray clouds that were steadily rolling over the valley and felt the first stir of fresh breeze on their faces. It was going to rain sometime this morning. They scattered to their various assignments.

At nine o'clock Seth finished hoeing the half acre of corn in the family garden, just as the first rain drops came plopping, making tiny volcanos in the dust. At ten o'clock Seth dodged off the street onto the loading dock at the Bishop's storehouse and stopped under the overhang to stomp the mud from his feet and shake the pounding rain from his coat and hair before he walked in.

Bishop Ezekiel Glade raised his head from his huge, leather bound ledger. "Seth, how are you?" He looked out over the tops of his glasses. "You're soaked."

"Fine, Bishop, fine. Looks like business is down today."

"Yep. Too wet and muddy out there."

"If you're not too busy, I thought it would be a good day to interview you."

Bishop Glade put down his feather quill pen. "Interview? For what?"

"Newspaper. You haven't heard?"

Bishop Glade shrugged. "No."

For five minutes Seth talked, gesturing, pacing, pointing. "So we intend interviewing a lot of businesses and writing editorials for Brother Dudley. What do you think?"

Bishop Glade chuckled. "Ought to keep you out of trouble. What do you want to know about the storehouse?"

Seth asked questions and hurriedly scribbled notes on a notepad for ten minutes, and then he asked, "Do you have many people come in who are not members of the church?"

"More and more every day. Lots of new people moving into the valley."

"Do you help them?"

"They're all our brothers and sisters. We help them if they're willing to help themselves. We won't rob a man of his self respect by making him a slave to free handouts."

"That's a great statement - it'll make good print." Seth scribbled furiously for a few seconds and then continued.

"Hawk thought you might have had two men come in yesterday that were not members of the church. He saw them at temple square. Did they get here?"

"Yes, matter of fact they did."

"Soldiers?"

"I think one used to be. Wore an army hat."

"Did you get their names?"

Bishop Glade turned back a page in his great ledger. "Watkins and Thomas."

Seth wrote some more. "Get their first names?"

"Jeremy and William."

"Are they coming back?"

"Not likely. I got their names and gave them a work assignment, but they left. I think they wanted a free handout. Life doesn't work that way."

"Right. Good point. That's good print," Seth said expertly, and scribbled again.

* * *

Abe and Jacob pushed open the front door of Dudley's newspaper office and stopped to scrape their muddy shoes on the iron boot scraper and shake the water from their coats.

"Mornin', Mr. Dudley."

"Morning, boys. That's fierce out there."

"Good for the spring crops," Abe said. "We're working on the editorial like you talked with Libby yesterday, but we got thinking. I'd like to learn to set type and how you work things in here. I'd do it for free, maybe during mornings. I'm good with my hands. I'd do a good job. Honest."

Dudley looked around. "You want to learn all this?"

"Yes sir. I sure do."

Dudley looked at Jacob.

"You too?"

"No sir. I'd like to learn how to be a good reporter."

Dudley shook his head and suddenly he laughed out loud. "You kids sure don't let grass grow under your feet. Sure. When do you want to start?"

"Right now."

* * *

Hawk sat in his shed with a blanket draped over his shoulders and listened to the steady drumming on the corrugated tin roof, and watched through the open door as the driving rain made mud and then puddles and then rivulets which ran to lower ground to form ponds. The rain made the temple stones and scaffolding too slippery and dangerous to work, and the crews had gone home to wait it out. Hawk sat lost in his own thoughts, silently listening, watching.

Movement in the torrential downpour caught his eye and he snapped alert and studied two shadowy shapes seventy yards away, walking south through temple square, heads bowed, shoulders hunched in the rain, as they picked their way through the rocks and skids and sawhorses scattered about on the grounds.

Suddenly he quickened. There was something familiar in the way one of the men walked. The thick one with the heavy shoulders. Something familiar . . .

He sat like a stone, unmoving while the two dim forms worked through the grounds, out into South Temple and continued towards State Street. Silently Hawk shed the blanket and slipped outside. He hunched his shoulders against the deluge and quickly worked his way across the street, down to State. He watched the two men cross at First East and continue east. In a moment Hawk was there, watching again as they crossed the street and entered a narrow passageway between the Delmonico Hotel and Dailey's Harness Shop. Hawk trotted across the street and slipped silently to the passageway and thrust his head around for a quick glance.

The narrow gap was covered, shielded from the rain. The first man had vanished and the second was just disappearing through a door that was nearly hidden from the street. It closed and Hawk waited for a moment before he moved quickly, silently down the dark passage and carefully twisted the door handle.

Locked.

Hawk dropped to one knee and studied the tracks left by the men in the moist dirt and his mouth became a straight line as he read them like a book.

The big shouldered man and the drinking man who had asked about the Bishop's storehouse yesterday! There was no mistaking the tracks made by their worn boots.

What were they doing moving about town in the rain? Who did they come to meet in this back room of Delmonico's Hotel?

Hawk trotted back to the street and crossed First East and stood on the board sidewalk in front of Quigley's hardware store, beneath the overhang, behind a barrel filled with pitchforks and rakes. The rain thinned, then came heavier. Minutes passed and nothing moved in the mud of the street, or on the sidewalk while Hawk watched and waited. A block east, a freighter cracked his whip and bellowed at twelve oxen pulling a giant freight wagon, their big hooves sinking deep into the rutted mud of the street at each step. The huge wagon rumbled on, and would pass in front of Hawk.

Then, the two men appeared from the dim shadows of the covered passageway, and behind them came a third, shorter, more slender man, younger than the others, carrying a black satchel under his arm. They stopped at the street and peered for a moment at the creeping freight wagon, and Hawk watched and listened to every move, every sound. The steady drumming of the rain muddled most of their brief talk, but Hawk understood two words as the men turned to go.

"After midnight."

Then they pulled their hatbrims lower against the rain and hurried up the street.

After midnight! What was to happen after midnight? Where?

Hawk darted from behind the barrel and started to follow, but the plodding oxen slowly pulled the great, muddy freight wagon in front of him and blocked his passage and Hawk stopped. If he ran around the back of the wagon, would he draw attention, be seen? He could not risk it. He waited impatiently while the wagon passed, and then he braced, eyes searching, ready to follow the three men.

They were gone, vanished as though by magic! Hawk settled back against the building front to watch for anything that moved, and there was nothing.

He trotted back across First East, into the passageway by the hotel, where he once again dropped to one knee and studied the tracks.

First the two that were familiar, and then the third set of tracks that he had not seen before, - those made by the new man.

* * *

Dudley looked at the big round clock above his cluttered desk.

"Abe, you were only going to work 'til noon. It's nearly four!"

"What? It can't be." Abe looked at the clock in amazement. "I got to get home. I got chores and horses to tend."

He set the mallet on the tabletop and looked at the twelve lines of letters he had carefully assembled under the watchful eye of Dudley. He drew and released a great breath.

"That's a good feeling," he said.

"Wait 'til you see it in print," Dudley said. "Something special about it when you see it in print."

Abe wiped at his hands with the big, stained towel. "How do you make fancy borders for things, like flyers and handbills, and money?"

"Engravings. Mostly from wood."

"You got any here?"

"Sure. You seen 'em on some of the handbills I've printed."

"Who makes those engravings? You?"

"No. It takes an engraver to do it right. It's a special art, that requires special tools. Fine tools."

"Mostly wood engravings? Are there other kinds?"

"Sure. Metal. They use metal engravings to print money and fine books."

"We got any good engravers in the valley?"

"Not yet. But soon. Why? Want to learn engraving?""

"Might." Abe looked out at the steadily falling rain. "I'm going to be wet before I get home this time," he said. "See you in the morning."

Jacob stopped on the board sidewalk in front of ZCMI long enough to scrape the mud from his shoes on the iron cleat bolted to the planks, then pushed his way into the nearly deserted store.

"May I help you, young man," an elderly sister said.

"Just came to talk with Mr. Zollinger. Is he here?"

"In his office at the back. What did you need to see him about?"

"I'm a newspaper reporter. I want to interview him."

The woman dropped her head forward and stared over her glasses.

"A newspaper reporter? Which newspaper?"

"Only one in town. Brother Dudley's. Deseret Examiner."

"Is Mr. Zollinger expecting you?"

"No, but he knows me. Jacob Pierce."

"We'll see," said the woman and quickly retreated to the rear of the store. A minute later George Zollinger came striding up the aisle between men's shirts and men's trousers.

"Jacob, you wanted to see me? What's this about a newspaper?"

"I'm reporting for Brother Dudley. I thought this might be a good day to take a minute, if you're not busy."

Zollinger shrugged. "Come on back."

Jacob was soon seated in the office, and pulled out his notebook and pencil.

"We're doing some articles on businesses, to see how they're doing with the new people moving in. Have you noticed any change in your business lately?"

"It's grown. We've also had some stealing."

"Oh? How serious?"

"It's getting more serious lately."

Jacob wrote on his notepad. "Are people bringing in new money?"

"Some are."

"Gold or paper money?"

"Some of each."

"Is the paper money good?"

"Most of it."

"Noticed any that wasn't? And who brings it in?"

"We've got a few bills here, yes."

"Could I see them?"

Zollinger opened the small safe in the corner of his office and removed a tin box. He unlocked it and dug out four bills, and handed them to Jacob. "Those are not good."

"Why? They look like they're okay."

"Counterfeit. They look like regular quartermaster notes drawn on the St. Louis government treasury, but they're phony. Good, but phony."

"Can't you get anything for them?", Jacob exclaimed.

Zollinger shrugged. "Worthless."

Jacob took one and held it to the light while he studied it. It was printed in green, edged with an orange border that looked like delicate ivy leaves. "Keeping these?"

"Yes, for evidence in case they catch the men who did it."

"Good idea. Okay, let's move on. What are your most popular items for sale in the store this spring?"

"Women's new fashions."

"Hi, Brother Charlie," Seth called.

"Howdy, Seth."

"How's the freighting business?"

Charlie glanced at the sky and the rain. "In this rain? What business? One freight wagon came in today, and that's all."

"Got a minute I can interview you?"

"Interview me? Am I lookin' for work?," Charlie said, and grinned.

Seth laughed. "No, I'm working with Brother Dudley at the newspaper office. We're interviewing some of the local businesses to see how things are going in the valley. That okay?"

"Sure. Drag up a barrel and set. We got a few minutes before five o'clock closeup."

"What's the most common stuff you handle here?"

"Women's fashions, and farming things, like plows and harnesses. Seed."

"Anything really heavy?"

"Once we had a boiler come in. Weighed eleven tons."

"You handle Dudley's printing press stuff?"

"Some of it. He hauled some direct in his own wagon."

"Any other printing stuff?"

"Naw." He scratched his jaw. "Come to think of it, a while back I got in a wood crate - better'n two hundred pounds - that was supposed to be cast iron skillets for the miners, but one of the slats was busted and I noticed the inside box was marked Acme Company, Boston, Mass, and then it said, Makers of Fine Printing Equipment. Musta been some kind of mistake."

"Who was it for?"

"Forgot the man's name."

"How long ago?"

"Maybe three, four months."

"Let's see. What else do we need to know. Oh yeah. You keep records of all this freight?"

"Sure."

"Could you total it up by months, to see if there's a steady increase in volume?"

"We do that already."

"Could I get those totals?"

"Sure. Come on back tomorrow."

"Could I see some of the original shipping receipts or whatever you call them?"

"The manifests?" Charlie shrugged. "Sure. Why not."

"Great. What time tomorrow?"

"Mid-afternoon's our slow time."

* * *

"Libby, you be careful out there in the rain and the dark. You go straight home."

Hilda Gunderson shook her finger sternly.

"I will," Libby said with her obedient smile. "I promise. And thank you loads for your help. You and the sisters are wonderful. We'll have this editorial finished ahead of schedule. Brother Dudley will be just thrilled."

Hilda smiled grandly. "Anything for the youth."

"I'll hurry. See you later."

Libby held an old newspaper over her head as she descended the front steps of the two storied, square, brick Gunderson home and turned north. The rain made a tat-tat-tat on the newspaper as she ran.

A movement ahead caught her eye and she slowed.

There! The figure of a man lurking in the trees and the bushes!

She gasped and her heart leaped. He's hiding! He has long scraggly hair! He's an assassin, waiting to murder me, or worse.

She spun to her right and darted between two houses, across the back yard, out onto third east, then sprinted south. She turned once more and her legs pumped hard as she ran for Seth's home. She took the front stairs two at a time and pounded on the door.

Elizabeth Dunn threw the door open and gasped, "Libby! In Heaven's name, child, you're terrified! Come in here this instant. What's happened?"

Fighting tears, Libby blurted, "I was going home . . Hilda's . . a man . ."

Seth came pounding into the room. "Libby!" he nearly shouted. "Has someone harmed you? Are you all right?"

"There's a man out there - - waiting for me - a murderer - or worse!"

She sagged against Seth and he caught her and held her up. Elizabeth fetched a chair and Seth helped Libby settle onto it.

"Did he touch you? Harm you?"

"No," she gasped. "I ran."

"Where was he?"

"Back by Hilda's. North of Hilda's."

Instantly Seth thought of Jacob and his rifle - - no time.

"Mama, take care of her. I'm going." Seth could hardly control the surge of anger that rose from deep in his soul.

Elizabeth Dunn planted herself firmly in front of the door. "You're not leaving here, young man, not if there's an assassin lurking out there."

"I'm going, mama," Seth said resolutely. "I've got to." He brushed past his mother and was gone before he could be stopped.

Seth sprinted harder than ever in his entire life. He

slowed when he passed the Gunderson home, and realized he had no stick, no club, no weapon to defend himself, but he didn't care. He walked briskly north, watching everything that moved in the steady rain. He took a firm hold on his anger, and tried to control his gasping from the run.

Nothing moved. He walked on, fast, ready.

Still nothing moved.

"Show yourself," he called. "Coward. Come on out and show yourself."

Nothing.

Then, from his right, from a peach tree surrounded by lilac bushes in the front yard of the Haslam home, came the soft call of a mourning dove.

Instantly Seth turned, arms half raised, ready, and then he remembered.

Check in with Porter every second day. Use the call of a mourning dove.

Brigham Young's advice.

Seth had forgotten!

Like an apparition from nowhere, the flat crowned hat and the rain soaked hair, and the square shoulders of Orrin Porter Rockwell appeared before Seth.

"Been lookin' fer yuh," the nasal voice twanged.

"Porter!" The unquenched anger in Seth's breast surged. "Porter, you scared Libby half to death. She . . ."

"Sorry, son," Porter cut in. "Didn't mean to. I been trackin' you five kids for two days. Lord knows it's kept me hoppin'. I just need one of you to tell me what's happenin'. Brigham needs to know."

Seth stopped and quieted. "It's my fault. I forgot to report. It won't happen again."

"Don't let it bother you. What's happening?"

For ten minutes Seth stood in the steady rain and talked while Porter listened intently to every word.

"And that's where we are," Seth finished. "I'll know

more in two days. I promise I'll find you and report."

"Do that. I'll tell Brigham what's going on. You kids are really stirrin' things up."

Even in the dark and the rain, Seth could see the grin on Porter's face.

"I don't think anybody has an idea what you're really doin' out there," Porter said. "Like a bunch of ghosts. Yer there, but nobody sees what yer doin'."

He paused. "Brigham's Ghost Brigade. Wish Lot Smith and me coulda had you kids out there on the prairie and in the canyons when Brigham assigned us to slow down the incoming army. Mighta turned 'em clear around."

Porter turned to go, then stopped. "Tell Libby I'm sorry clean to my bones about scarin' her. I'll try hard to never do that again. That girl's pure wheat."

Four

HAWK STIRRED, THEN SAT bolt upright on his low bunk inside his shed, suddenly tense, wide awake. For a moment he wondered what had wakened him, then realized. It was the silence. The rain had stopped, and with it, the steady drumming of on the tin roof.

Was it midnight?

He threw back the blanket he had wrapped around his shoulders for warmth while he waited for midnight, and was out the door, moving across the deserted temple square like a shadow. He glanced at the heavens, where a rift in the clouds showed a myriad of twinkling stars. He passed the town clock on the ZCMI corner - 11:50 - and continued at a trot down the deserted street, and turned left. He stopped on the boardwalk in front of Quigleys hardware store, across from the Delmonico hotel, and settled down in the doorway, lost in the shadows.

At two o'clock a breeze came down from Emigration canyon and Hawk wrapped his arms around himself to keep from shivering. At two thirty he stood to flex his legs and move his arms to try to keep warm. At three o'clock he rose and started back towards First East, then quickly leaped back into the doorway. He closed his eyes to concentrate, and listened for the faint sound that had turned him. There it was again, and suddenly he recognized it. The sound of a horse or mule slogging in the street mud.

Who would be walking a horse or a mule down First East at four o'clock in the morning? And why?

He breathed slowly and remained a statue. Whoever was leading the animal would not see him, but the animal, even in the dark, might sense him if he made a sound, or a move.

Suddenly they were there, angling across the street towards the hotel; three men hunched furtively, heads turning, the middle one leading a large mule with a pack saddle and tarp tied to its back. They stopped in front of the dark passageway at the side of the hotel and one man held the lead rope on the mule while the other two disappeared.

Minutes passed. The mule moved its feet and the man took the cheekstrap on the halter and talked low to settle the animal. He turned to look all directions to be certain he had not been seen.

From the dark passageway, one man, then the other emerged, carrying a canvas-wrapped bundle between them, grunting softly with the weight of it. They sloshed into the muddy street and held the bundle next to the mule while the third man quickly slipped the looped ropes on the bundle over the prongs of the pack saddle, and then tied it on one side of the mule.

Hawk strained to see their faces or their build, but they remained only black figures in the darkness of the overcast heavens.

Again two men disappeared, and Hawk waited. They

returned with a second bundle, and tied it on the other side of the mule. They covered the load with the tarp, and then stood silently for several seconds while they listened. Hawk peered intently from the dark doorway. For a moment the full moon shone through a break in the ragged clouds and caught them full in the face.

Hawk's breathing stopped for a second when recognition struck into his brain. They were the three who had been there earlier, and left with a black satchel!

There was no sound, no movement in the broad expanse of the street. Satisfied no one had seen them, they led the mule east, up the street.

Hawk counted twenty breaths before he slipped off the boardwalk and picked his way through the mud, following them. For twenty minutes they zigzagged south and east to the outskirts of town, and finally stopped behind a spacious, two storied building. There was not a single light in the building. Every window was black.

Sister Olson's boarding house! What were they doing at a boarding house with a loaded pack mule, at four thirty in the morning?

Patiently Hawk watched as they silently lifted one of the heavy bundles from the pack saddle and carried it up the back stairs and disappeared, and then returned for the other bundle. They made no light, and no sound.

Then two of them returned, tied the empty, folded tarp back onto the pack mule, and quickly retraced their path back towards town.

Hawk glanced at the sky, then the eastern rim of the Wasatch mountains. The clouds were breaking, and streaks of gray were showing, heralding the coming of the sunrise. Hawk waited until the men were out of sight before he broke a branch from a juniper tree and sprinted to the bottom of the back stairway. For a moment he knelt to study the muddy prints on the ground, and then on the steps. The new man was the one who had remained inside Widow Olson's boarding house. The other two had led the mule away.

Hawk backed away from the stairs and used the juniper branch to carefully brush away his tracks. They would be too clear after the rain; he did not want to be detected. Then he sprinted after the two men as the scattering clouds turned pink, and in minutes he caught sight of the men as the reds and golds of sunrise pierced the heavens. He slowed as they turned back onto State Street, and slowed again when he peered around the corner. They had stopped to re-tie the tarp on the pack saddle so it would not appear they had just finished unloading; they were afraid someone in the streets might see them.

Hawk stopped. He dared go no further until they did. If they saw him . . .

He waited. They moved on and he followed, always out of sight. They continued towards temple square, then turned west, two blocks, and headed for Smith's livery. They disappeared in the huge barn, then minutes later walked back onto the street without the mule or pack saddle. They spoke for a moment, then separated, one quickly heading north, the other south.

Hawk could follow neither without being seen.

Quickly he ran back to the Delmonico hotel and once more knelt in the dark passageway and examined the tracks. The new prints of the two men were much deeper than the old.

"It was heavy," he said to himself. "Whatever they moved to Widow Olson's, it was heavy."

He straightened and darted back to the street and headed east, then south. He was going to be late for the five o'clock meeting at the well house behind the Ward building.

* * *

Seth tossed the scoop back into the feed bin and

watched for a second while Old Boxer and the hens came pecking for the scattered grain, and then Seth headed south. He glanced about and slowed.

The rain had freshened every growing thing in the valley. The fruit trees on each lot sparkled. Seth could see the round, full fruit in the green leaves, growing, maturing. The yards and the shrubs and the flowers were green and gold and red, and he glanced down the valley through the clean, crystal clear air, and could see as far as the west shores of Utah Lake.

"Brigham was right!," he exclaimed aloud. "This is the place. We can have heaven right here. The only thing we need is time, and work, and if the Lord will grant us one, we can do the other."

He felt a deep, secure, solid pride in his people, and what they had done, and what they would yet do, as he worked his way south and east. He wondered if it was unrighteous pride, but threw the thought aside. He only knew that this morning the world was bright and beautiful, and he thrilled at being alive in this place, and he picked up his stride.

Ten minutes later he slowed at the well house.

"Where's Hawk," he asked, panting.

"Don't know," Abe said. "Haven't seen him since yesterday."

"Okay, we'll start without him. Abe, you first."

Abe reported, then Jacob, Libby, and finally Seth, who began to pace.

"I'm worried about Hawk. It's not like . ." He stopped and sighed with relief as Hawk came trotting around the Ward house.

"You had us worried," Seth said.

"What happened?"

For five minutes Hawk told them about the three men, and the visit to the hotel and then Olson's boarding house.

"Hummm," Seth said as he resumed pacing. "Let's put

all this together."

He pursed his mouth and tugged at his upper lip. "We know that to print money you must have engravings, and to get engravings you have to have an engraver, but Dudley doesn't know of any engravers in town. We know the counterfeit money was printed with green and orange ink. We know that some time back someone shipped in some stuff through the freight office that was supposed to be cast iron skillets but it was manufactured in Boston by a company that makes printing equipment."

He paused to collect the rest of his thoughts.

"We know that two suspicious men named Watkins and Thomas got a third man from Delmonicos, and in the middle of the night the three of them packed something heavy on a mule and unloaded it at Olson's boarding house, and we know the third man took a black satchel somewhere earlier."

He pulled his lip again. "I think we've got to find out who that third man is and what's in that satchel, and if we can, what was carried up to the second floor of Olson's at four o'clock this morning."

He stopped and faced the other four. "So here's what we do. I'll check those freight bills at Charlie's, and Abe, you find out from Dudley how someone would get green and yellow ink. Jacob, you go on down to Delmonico's and see if you can interview Brother Kendrick about the hotel business, and find out if he has someone there who fits Hawk's description of that third man. Young, slender, you know."

He turned to Libby. "You go interview Sister Olson, like you're trying to find out about how her boarding house business is, with all the new people moving into the valley. Maybe you can find out about what went up into the second floor of the boarding house last night."

Libby nodded.

Seth paused. "You okay after your scare last night?"

Libby nodded again.

"What scare," Jacob demanded, and rose to his feet.

"Nothing," Seth said.

Libby's head thrust forward. "Nothing? If I'd had a gun he would have been dead! Nothing, you say?"

Jacob rose to one knee. "Someone threatened Libby?"

"It was my fault," Seth said defensively. "I told you last night, I forgot to report. Porter felt bad; said you were pure wheat."

Jacob's face puckered. "Pure wheat?"

"Just Porter's way of saying she's fine."

"Pure wheat? Is that guy crazy?"

Seth chuckled. "No, he's just Orrin Porter Rockwell. He said something else that you might want to hear. He said we're doing this job for the Prophet, but nobody knows it, like we're all ghosts. He called us Brigham's Ghost Brigade."

Abe cocked his head. "I like it," he said.

"Me too," said the others nearly in unison.

"So do I," Seth answered. "Now let's get at it."

As they walked away, Seth said to Hawk, "You better get some sleep. You didn't get much last night."

Hawk shrugged. "I got some tracks to look at."

* * *

Jacob tapped the bell on the hotel clerk's desk and it dinged loudly, and he stood savoring the pungent smells of fried ham and eggs and pancakes drifting in from the restaurant. The clerk scurried in and sized up Jacob with a critical eye.

"Yes, can I help you?"

Jacob held up his pencil and notepad and smiled broadly. "Jacob Pierce from the Examiner. I'd like to talk with Brother Kendrick about a lot of free publicity in the newspaper. Is he around?"

The clerk looked dubious, but hooked a thumb back towards the restaurant. "Eating breakfast."

Jacob didn't wait for an invitation, but strode quickly

through the large, glass paned double doors and stopped inside. In a moment he spied Elias Kendrick seated in a corner table with another man, who put down his cup and wiped his face with a clean, freshly ironed napkin. He said something to Kendrick and rose and walked out the double doors.

Jacob walked to the table.

"Good morning, Brother Kendrick," he said with a huge smile. "I'm working with Brother Dudley at the newspaper, gathering stuff for an editorial about business in the valley. Your hotel is an important place, with all the new people you see every day. Got a minute?"

"An editorial?"

"Yep. Second page. A lot of free publicity for you."

Kendrick's eyes brightened. "How can I help?"

"Business up lately?"

Kendrick reflected. "Yes, a little. Quite a bit, matter of fact."

"Keep records on it?"

"Yes, every month."

"What kind of people take rooms here? Are we getting doctors, or harness makers, or drifters, or what?"

"The hotel register shows the company they're with, but they don't always fill it out."

"Anyone move in or move out the past couple days? Or did the rain slow your business down like everybody else?"

"Matter of fact it did. We had a man move out yesterday, but nobody moved in. Seems like the rain stopped people from travelling."

"How long does the average guest stay?"

"Depends. We have some back rooms we rent by the week, others by the day. Depends."

"The man that moved out, was he by the day or by the week?"

"By the week. Two weeks, to be exact. Paid his bill early this morning."

"How about the restaurant. Any change?"

"Generally business is good. The rain slowed it down but it'll pick up. We served nearly a full house this morning."

"Great! Any chance I could glance at the register?"

Kendrick shrugged. "Just a glance, but you can't use any names of any guests in your editorial."

"Sure. Thanks," Jacob said, and followed him back to the clerk's desk. Kendrick watched while Jacob studied the entries in the large register.

"These people all still here?"

Kendrick looked. "No, some are gone."

"Here's a couple that listed ZCMI. Know who they were?"

"Robert J. Barton and wife. Said he was here to sell dry goods."

"Here's one with no company listed. He still here?"

"John Jones. No, he's the one that paid and left this morning."

"Oh. Young man?"

"Why are you interested in that?"

Jacob shrugged. "No reason. Young man with no company listed, just thought he might be a drifter or something."

"He was in a back room. Stayed two weeks. Ran some sort of a business; he had some tools in a black bag. He had visitors."

"Oh. What visitors? What kind of business?"

"Mostly two men. And a salesman or two."

"Did the salesmen check into the hotel?"

"No, just came to sell things."

"What kind of things?"

"I don't know. Not my business to know."

"Sure. What about this man?"

"Seed salesman."

"Good. Uh, Mr. Kendrick, would it be possible to look at a couple of your empty rooms, one for overnight and another one by the week? Might mean a lot of business if I could describe them."

* * *

"Hi, Charlie! Find those receipts?" Seth jumped up onto the freight platform.

"Manifests? Yep, right over there on the desk. Come on."

Seth followed Charlie across the floor of the freight house to the cluttered desk in the corner.

"Good. Let's take a look."

It took three minutes to find the manifest that stated two men, Jackson and Smith, had picked up one crate of cast iron skillets, shipped by Acme Manufacturing Company out of Boston.

"Those the guys that got the skillets?," Seth asked.

"Yep. Said they were going to sell 'em to miners."

"What did these two look like?"

Charlie scratched his head. "Well now, let me see, seems like one of them was heavy in the shoulders, kinda thick in the neck, and the other'n was skinnier, and had a red nose, like he was a drinker. Know what I mean?"

"The prophet's right. Drink is not for man."

"Someone should of told that one gent that a long time ago."

Seth sorted through several more papers, made some notes, and shook Charlie's hand.

"Thanks a lot. I'll see your name shows up in the editorial."

Charlie beamed. "Well now, that's right neighborly."

"Brother Dudley, you use only black ink?" Abe paused to wipe his hands on the big, ink stained rag.

"Yes. Well, mostly. Why?"

"If we wanted to do something real fancy, like with engravings, could you get other colors?"

"Sure."

"Blues and reds and greens and yellows?"

"Got to order them from St. Jo or St. Louis, and it takes a little time. But it can be done."

Hawk walked in the cavernous livery barn, over to the desk where Nephi McKesson was sitting. Nephi was leaned over a ledger, eyes closed, breathing deeply, his quill pen fallen from his fingers.

"Mornin' Brother Gregg," Hawk said softly.

Nephi's head snapped up and he mumbled, "What's that you say," and shook his head until his eyes focused.

"Oh. Hawk. Scared me half to death. Must have dozed off. What can I do for you?"

"We've got a youth project going and . . ."

"I heard about it. Yessir. I heard."

"Might need something to carry newspapers down to the south end of the valley once a week. What you got?"

"A buggy, or a pack mule. Why can't you use old Dudley's rig for that?"

"Might be too much of a load. Mind if I look around?"

"Not at all."

Hawk walked down one side of the barn, looking into the stalls where horses and mules were tied, then started back up the other side, and stopped.

"Here's a mule that might do the job. Say, didn't I see this one in the streets this morning?"

"Probably did. Two fellas rented old Daisy last night."

"How much for one day?"

"Hummm. Well, for you kids, one dollar."

"Who were the men who rented her? Will they want her again?"

"Names were Baker and Kelly, as I remember. Naw, that was a one time deal. They won't rent her again."

Hawk studied the tracks of the mule for a moment, then continued on back to the big doors.

"Thanks for your time, Brother Gregg. If we need a mule, I'll know where to come."

* * *

"Sister Olson! How nice to see you." Libby's smile was dazzling. "Libby," Sister Olson exclaimed while she wiped her hands in her apron, "what a surprise. What brings you to a boarding house?"

"May I come in?"

"Of course."

Libby followed Sigrid into the parlor and stopped and raised her nose.

"My, what is that lovely fragrance? Is that berry pie, by chance?"

Sigrid flushed. "Yes. Baking for supper."

Libby shook her head. "You have very fortunate guests, Sister Olson. That's partly why I'm here."

"Oh?"

"Yes. You see, we have a youth project . ."

"I've heard."

"Sister Hilda?"

"Most of the sisters are talking about it."

"How nice. We're writing an editorial for Brother Dudley. We're visiting some of the more prominent businesses, and yours is among them."

Sigrid's jaw dropped. "It is?"

"Of course. Where better to get information about who is coming and going in our valley?"

"Well, now that you mention it . . ."

"Do you usually have your rooms filled?"

"Usually, yes."

"Do your boarders have jobs in town?"

"Yes, a lot of them just stay here until they can move their families here, into a home. And, we have some single people who don't want to bother with keeping up a home."

"How interesting. Are your rooms filled now?"

"All but one."

"Have you rented any out lately?"

"Yes, to a young man upstairs."

"Oh. A nice young man, I'm sure."

Sigrid shrugged. "Seems nice enough, but I'm not too sure about his friends."

"I'm sorry to hear that. Is there a problem?"

"No, they just don't look like the kind I'd like here."

"Well, I hope they don't bother you. It would be so nice to be able to see one or two of your rooms so I can describe how clean and healthful they are in the article. But I suppose that is asking too much."

"Oh not at all," Sigrid said quickly. "Come, we'll look at one or two."

Libby followed her down the long hall on the main floor, examined two clean, tidy rooms, then upstairs to the second floor, where they looked at two more.

"That gives you an idea of the rooms," Sigrid said.

Libby pointed to room number eight. "Is that the room taken by the new young man?"

"Yes."

"I'm sure he's there, isn't he?"

"No. He left this morning with his black bag and hasn't come back yet."

"Isn't that the corner room?"

"Yes."

"Could I see a corner room? Maybe not this one."

Sigrid drew a key from her apron pocket. "I'm sure he won't mind," she said, and opened the locked door.

Sigrid held the door while Libby walked into the room and quickly looked around.

The bed was rumpled and some clothes were tossed over a chair; otherwise there was nothing remarkable in the room. But there was a faint essence in the air. For a split second she closed her eyes and concentrated. Where have I smelled that smell before?

She could not remember. She walked back into the hall. "Before I leave, could I look into your kitchen? When I describe your berry pie, you'll have people wanting to rent just to eat at your table."

* * *

The ZCMI town clock said 2:20 A.M. when Hawk trotted down State Street, dark and deserted. He turned east on seventh south and continued to Olson's boarding house. He crept silently down the hedge of lilacs on the north side, and parted the green branches and the white and purple blossoms to peer at the corner room on the second floor, just above the stairs.

The window curtains were closed, and something had been hung hung over them, perhaps a blanket or a sheet, but there was a light inside. The window glowed dully.

Hawk circled the entire house.

It was the only room with a light burning.

Hawk glided silently back to the street and continued back towards Temple Square, retracing his steps. In the full moonlight he could see his own tracks, and suddenly, he stopped.

There were fresh tracks beside his own. He dropped to one knee and in the silvery moonlight thrust his face low to study them.

He had been followed!

He moved a little further and again dropped to his knees to peer closely.

Whoever was following him had a right leg that was slightly shorter than the left.

Quickly Hawk darted to the side of the street, back up the boardwalk, up first east, then cut through a vacant lot, scaled a high board fence, and turned once again back toward Olson's boarding house.

He studied his tracks at the boarding house carefully. There were no other fresh tracks.

The man had not followed him that far.

Why was he following only part way across town?

And who was he?

Hawk moved like a shadow, straight west past State Street, to Second West, then north, and came onto Temple Square from the west side. He listened for ten minutes, and watched in the pale, silvery moonlight.

There was no one.

Five

"OKAY," SETH SAID, AND pulled his lip while he paced. "We all know where we are. We got the man in Olson's boarding house working on something in the middle of the night, and Libby smelled something in his room that she's smelled before but can't remember. We got a man with a bad right leg following Hawk, we got two men using Baker and Taylor and Watkins and Thomas and a lot of other fake names, and we got two men who picked up some printing equipment at Charlie's a couple months ago. Was it the same two guys?"

He stopped and stood erect and heaved a great sigh. "Well, we're just going to have to wait on some of the answers because we got to get this editorial done, like we promised. And we got to get the night patrols organized and then we split up to cover the first five wards Sunday to get the kids assigned. Just two days."

He scratched his jaw. "I got your notes, so I'll write the editorial. Libby, you and Jacob and Abe get around and make a list of all the kids in the nine wards. We'll meet at nine in the morning at my place and I'll read you the editorial and we'll all correct it and Libby and I will deliver it to Dudley." "Okay so far?"

Everyone nodded silent approval.

"Hawk, you circulate through town looking for the tracks of that man with one short leg. If those counterfeiters have figured this out and are tracking us, we could be in real trouble. So if you find them, come get me and I'll get Porter. I reported to him last night, and I know how to find him."

They separated their separate ways, Libby walking beside Jacob back towards her home.

"Isn't he wonderful," she said, and looked at Jacob from the corners of her eyes.

"Who?"

"Seth." She cocked her head a little and looked wistful.

Jacob grimaced. "Yeah. Just wonderful. He's going to get us all killed."

Then he softened and looked at Libby. "Yes, he's good. My best friend."

Libby slipped her hand into Jacob's for a few paces, then broke free and turned on her street without a word, and Jacob stood stock still staring after her, totally befuddled.

Seth's wonderful, so she holds my hand. Now just what . . how do you figure . . . women, he finally said, and marched on.

Seth wore out one pencil and half of another one before he finally pushed himself back from the desk in his small room and stood and stretched stiff, set muscles.

"Seth, time for chores, and then supper" he heard from the parlor.

He blew air in amazement! It couldn't be that late. He walked downstairs and looked at the big clock on the carved mantle above the fireplace. Just past six o'clock.

Impossible!

He strode out and grained the chickens and dropped the whey from the morning milk into the trough for Betsy and her piglets, and walked Mossie into the milking barn. He guided her into her stantion and dropped a little grain and hay in the manger, and Mossie shoved her nose into it and began to munch.

He washed her bag, and settled the one legged milking stool on the ground on her right side, and slipped the shiny steel milk bucket beneath her, and said, "Good girl, good girl" as he balanced on the one legged stool and leaned his head into her flank and began working with his hands.

The first dozen squirts of warm, rich milk made pinging sounds as they struck the bottom of the bucket, and then the rich froth rose to quiet the sound as the bucket filled.

Seth set the full bucket on the milking table nearby, pushed the milking stool beneath it, opened the stantion, and said, "Good girl." He poured the milk into two pans to cool, as Mossie finished the last of the hay and slowly backed out of the stantion and sauntered back into the pen, to feed and water.

Seth carried the two pans to the root cellar behind the house and set them on a shelf in the cool dampness, and walked back to the milking shed. Ten minutes later he had washed the milk bucket and set it upside down on the milking table and cleaned out the stantion.

He whistled as he walked to the back porch, rolled up his sleeves, washed his hands and face, ducked over slightly to see himself in a piece of mirror while he ran a comb through his hair once, and walked into the kitchen.

"What's for supper?"

He sat down to ham, mashed potatoes, beet greens, milk, and a piece of chocolate cake, blessed the meal, and took a giant pile of mashed potatoes, covered with gravy.

"We got a letter today from your father," his mother said, and set it on the table beside Seth's plate.

He laid down his fork and picked up the envelope and held it in his hands for long seconds.

LONDON ENGLAND the postmark said. Reverently Seth opened the envelope and read:

"My Dear Ones:

I must first say, I miss you both, every day I am alive. I remember how beautiful it is in the valley at this time of year and I close my eyes and I am there, with you.

The work is going well here. Oh, many will not listen to us, but the Spirit is working, and some are secretly coming to our door at night to ask. We baptized four last Saturday night, in a river, after dark. They talked to others, and more and more are beginning to attend our street meetings.

My health is good, my spirits high. England is beautiful in the spring. London is a bustling town with many good people.

How grateful I am to both of you for your sacrifice in letting me answer the call of the Prophet to serve in this Mission. Great blessings will be yours, forever.

I know this is the Lord's work. I testify it to you. When I am back, it will be Seth's turn for his mission.

I pray for your safety and happiness every day. May God bless and keep you until my return.

Your faithful and loving husband and father, George Haslam Dunn."

Seth read it again, and carefully folded it and slipped it back into the envelope. He opened a cupboard drawer and tied it in the bundle of letters they had received from his father.

Seth looked at his mother, standing by the stove, puttering with the pots and pans, and he walked to her and put his arms about her.

"It's fine, mother. Don't cry." Margaret Dunn had nearly died giving birth to Seth. The doctor had been forced to do an operation that night. She could bear no more children, and the greatest hope, greatest dream in her life had been to give her husband a large family. In her heart of hearts, she sometimes felt she had somehow betrayed him.

She faced Seth and straightened and forced a brave smile while she wiped tears.

President Young had called her husband to serve a mission in England. She had not wavered. She took in sewing, and she and Seth worked the orchard and garden and sold fresh and bottled fruit. Seth did odd jobs for anyone he could. They raised pigs and a calf for winter's meat, and had Mossie for milk and cream, and they made cheese and sold part of it. Somehow, somehow there was always just enough, and a little to send to her beloved husband on his mission.

"Of course it's fine, son. I'm so grateful for your father and you."

She started to clear the table. "What have you been working on in your room all day," she asked, as she carried the dishes to the dishpan.

"The editorial for Brother Dudley."

It was past ten o'clock before Seth quit correcting the editorial and laid the pencil down. He went downstairs and knelt beside the huge bed in the master bedroom, beside his mother.

" . . and bless and protect father . . ."

At 8:55 the next morning Seth put the last touch on the editorial, and at nine o'clock he heard the sounds of feet on the front porch and glanced out at the Brigade.

"Come on around to the back porch," he said.

It took him fifteen minutes to read the seven page editorial. When he stopped, the others were wide-eyed, spellbound. Jacob looked incredulous and turned to Abe, then Libby. "Did we get all that stuff?"

"You sure did," Seth said. "What do you think?"

"It's great," Libby said, "but I don't know. Mr. Dudley might think it's too long."

Seth was deflated. "Think so? Maybe I should cut it down."

"You can't," Abe said. "It'll ruin it. Let's go with it that way."

"Hawk?"

"Good. Use it."

"You guys got those ward lists?"

Libby handed him five separate sheets and Seth looked them over.

"Hey, what's this in the fourth Ward? Sixteen kids named Smith?"

Jacob shrugged. "Brother Harley Smith's got three wives."

Seth's eyebrows arched. "Okay. I'll take the 5th ward. It's furthest south. Hawk, you take the first ward, up by Temple Square. You others divide the other lists."

He folded his list and stuffed it in his shirt pocket.

"Libby, you talked with Brother Dudley first. You coming with me to see if this editorial is okay?"

They all started their separate ways, Libby striding beside Seth.

"Isn't he wonderful," she said, and looked at him out of the corners of her eyes.

"Who's wonderful?"

"Jacob." She cocked her head wistfully.

Seth smiled. "He's good. One of my best friends."

She reached for his hand just as he folded the editorial and stuffed it in his shirt pocket, and he did not see the gesture. It fell unnoticed, and Libby looked chagrined.

They walked into the Desert Examiner office and Brother Dudley paused at his press.

"Morning. How's the editorial coming?"

"Finished," Seth said, and proudly fished it from his shirt pocket and handed it to Dudley.

Old Brother Dudley was frozen in his tracks.

"Uh, how . . . hand me that."

Slowly he counted the pages.

Suddenly Libby grasped Seth's arm and leaned close. "I remember I remember!," she hissed in his ear.

Seth looked at her with his nose wrinkled. "Remember what?" he whispered.

"Never mind," she whispered back. "Later."

Dudley finished his count and raised his face.

"Seven pages, front and back."

Seth licked dry lips. "Too long?"

"For an editorial? Yes, five times too long."

Seth sighed and his chin fell.

"Well," Dudley said, and tugged at his ear, "too long for an editorial, but not for a feature article."

Seth's head jerked up. "A what?"

"Feature article. By line. An article, by Seth Dunn."

"No sir, not by me," Seth said. "Five of us. You name one, you name us all."

"I already had the newspaper blocked. This is a new half page. Where do I put it?"

"I'm sure sorry, Mr. Dudley. I didn't . . we're so new at this."

A chuckle rolled up from Dudley's ample belt line. "I should have known. Okay. We'll go with it. We'll call it an Editorial because that's what we promised. I'll find some way to fill up the bottom half of the page."

"You will?," Seth blurted.

"Next time, one fourth this size. Understand?" Dudley looked over the tops of his glasses, from beneath the green visor that made his forehead look gray-green.

"Yes sir. I surely do."

Dudley smiled. "Not bad." He raised the document. "Matter of fact, pretty good. Should double the circulation for this issue. You got your groups ready to go sell this edition?"

"Yes sir, we do."

"Okay. I'll have it next week. Abe coming in Monday?"

"He surely is."

"Good. I got to get busy."

Seth led Libby out the front door and the instant the door was closed she grasped his arm with a death grip.

"I remembered!," she cried. "In there, I remembered."

"Remembered what?"

"The smell! The one I smelled in that man's room in Olson's boarding house. Remember?"

Seth searched his memory. "Oh, yeah. When you were interviewing Sister Olson."

"It was printer's ink. That's what I smelled up there. Printer's ink!"

"You sure?"

"Certain. Absolutely."

Seth stopped. "What was he doing up there with printer's ink?"

Libby shrugged. "I don't know."

Seth tugged his upper lip as he started walking towards home. "I'll figure a way to find out."

He waved to Libby where she turned on Main to go to meet her father at City Hall, and Seth trotted on to his own home. He had milk to churn for butter, and cheese, and curds and whey.

In the late twilight, when the sun was half hidden by the Oquirrh Mountains, Hawk walked from the Deseret Bank building back towards Temple Square. It was getting late, and he swallowed at the thought of herb tea and smoked elk meat and fresh turnips. He could have the simple meal ready five minutes after he got to his shed.

He stepped off the boardwalk into the dust of the wide

street and waited for the early Saturday night traffic to open as he worked his way across the street. He stepped up onto the boardwalk on the east side of the street and stopped.

He pivoted and stepped back into the street and dropped to one knee.

The tracks! The man with a short right leg, who had been following him.

He glanced the direction the tracks led, and could see no one who could have made them. Patiently he followed, and the tracks showed the man had stepped onto the boardwalk, and Hawk lost them.

With the patience of a tracker, he carefully walked on up the street, watching the tracks next to the boardwalk to see if the man stepped off again.

There! At the corner! He had crossed the street.

Hawk followed the trail, to Welles bakery, across the street to Utley's Gunsmith shop, then on north. Hawk followed until he was certain the tracks led back towards Temple Square, then turned south and ran. Ten minutes later, in late dusk, he rounded the corner into Seth's milking shed where Seth had just picked up the first of the two big steel bowls of milk.

"Hawk, what's happened," Seth exclaimed.

"I found the tracks of the man who followed me."

"Grab that other bowl of milk and follow me," Seth said, and they hurried to the root cellar and put the bowls on the shelf. Hawk led and Seth followed him at a run.

Ten minutes later Hawk stopped on State Street, just short of South Temple Street and pointed. "There. Those are his tracks."

"Sure?"

"That's him."

"Stay here. I'll be right back."

Seth sprinted a block east and scaled the fence that

enclosed the Lion House, with its twenty gables, and the immense Beehive House where Brigham lived. He dropped into the yard and paused to see if he had been seen, then trotted towards the carriage house at the rear of the lot. He stopped, then whistled low and soft, the call of the mourning dove.

"Lookin' for me," the familiar nasal voice twanged from the carriage shed.

Seth trotted over to the open doorway, and looked inside where Porter had the wheel off a light buggy, the axle blocked up while he dobbed thick axle grease on the stub end.

"Hawk found the tracks of the man who followed him," Seth panted.

Porter jammed the stick into the grease bucket and grabbed his gunbelt from a barrel top and buckled it on. He adjusted the two pistols, then clapped his hat on his head.

"Lead the way," he said.

Ten minutes later Seth slowed as they rounded the corner onto State Street. Hawk was waiting.

"Hawk, this is Orrin Porter Rockwell."

Hawk nodded and pointed at footprints in the dirt. "Those are the tracks."

Porter looked at them, and then leaned forward to look closer. He straightened and a broad grin split his face. Then he began to chuckle, and in a moment people were stopping to stare as he roared great gales of laughter.

Seth looked at Porter, then at Hawk, and shrugged. The two boys waited until Porter slowly recovered and finally drew and exhaled a great breath.

"That's the best joke this year! If that don't beat all. Boys, those tracks are mine!"

Hawk looked at Seth, and Seth looked at Porter, and then Seth began to laugh, and Hawk shook his head and could not hold back a smile. "You mean," Seth said, "you been tracking Hawk?"

"I mean I been tracking all you kids to watch out you don't get hurt. Brigham's orders." His shoulders shook in silent mirth, and he turned and started back to the Lion House and the two boys followed.

"I got to get back. They figure to use that buggy for church in the mornin'. I got to tell you kids, you sure cover a lot of country."

He stopped and looked at Hawk. "You remembered those tracks from the other day?"

Hawk nodded.

"When did you see 'em?"

"In the dark. Maybe three o'clock in the morning."

"Full moon?"

"Yes."

Porter's eyes narrowed as he studied the boy. "That's the work of a master tracker."

Seth interrupted. "He only made one mistake. He said your right leg was shorter than your left."

Porter's jaw dropped. "You read the tracks that way?"

"Yes."

"You're right. It is."

Hawk shrugged and Seth turned inquisitive eyes to Porter.

"Your right leg is short?"

"Yep. Happened when I was a boy. Walk along, I'll tell you about it."

The three of them walked across the street, headed east on South Temple, towards the high fence by the Eagle Gate.

"You see, I was born in Hampshire County Massachusetts in 1813, and when I was four my folks moved to Manchester County, New York. Two years later Joseph Smith's family moved in about a mile away.

That's when I met Joseph. When I was about ten I busted my right leg jumping off a barn and a doctor in Palmyra set it, but he set it crooked. Been a little shorter than my left ever since. No one much notices, except me."

He paused to look at Hawk. "And this boy."

He continued. "Joseph broke his leg too, and a doctor from Palmyra set his, and a bone splinter got infected inside. The doctor operated and got the splinter out, but it left Joseph with a little limp, too."

A smile crossed his face. "So me and Joseph, we both had a little limp from broken legs. I often wondered if it was the same doctor that did such a poor job setting our bones. I should of gone back to find out, and if it was, I should of talked to him a little stern."

He sobered. "Anyway, Joseph and I became fast friends. The best. I wish you could of known him then. He was something special, Joseph was. I cut cordwood and picked berries and done everything I could all summer to help pay for the first printing of the Book of Mormon. I listened to him tell about those plates a hundred times or more. He was special. An honest man couldn't be around him long before he knew Joseph was telling the truth. He could speak straight from his heart to yours."

He continued walking in silence for a moment.

"I stuck with him. Through it all, I was there with him. Went to jail for him, nearly got myself killed for him, and I'd do it all again. He was the voice of the Almighty, Joseph was."

He cleared his throat. "I got this long hair on account of Joseph. Once he prophesied, and told me that if I would not cut my hair, I would never be killed by an enemy. I knew he was a prophet of God so I listened. I haven't cut my hair from that day, and I been shot at by guns and arrows and three times men tried to knife me in the back, but none of them succeeded. Joseph was a prophet."

He stopped by the gate through the high wall enclosing the Beehive House and the Lion House. "It was just like with Jesus. Joseph was telling the world too many hard truths and they couldn't stand it, so they killed him. But Joseph had prepared Brigham, and I stayed right on with him. Nauvoo, Missouri, right on through all the killings and the burnings, and the persecutions. I was on the tail gate of that last wagon when we crossed the Missouri River ice when they drove us out, with my rifle cocked. Brigham told me to hold off the mob until we were all safely across that frozen river. I did it."

Seth saw the distant look in his eyes, even in the late shadows of dusk.

"We come west, me scouting, Brigham organizing, leading, inspiring the saints when things was so bad. I swear, sometimes I thought I was listening to Joseph again."

He reached for the gate handle.

"And it's starting up all over. Brigham's too strong. There's men who want to bring him down because they're afraid of him. But they won't if I can help it."

He stopped and drew a deep breath.

"That's the longest speech I made since I can remember. Hope it didn't bore you two men."

Seth stood dumbfounded, and could only shake his head.

Porter turned to Hawk. "You read my short leg in my tracks in the dark?"

Hawk nodded.

"That's the best tracking I ever heard of and I done my share of tracking. I'll remember."

Six

SETH PACED WITH HIS head bowed, forehead wrinkled in deep thought, then suddenly straightened and jabbed a finger towards the early morning sky.

"I've got it," he exclaimed.

"Got what," Jacob asked.

"A pain," replied Abe.

The four of them sat breathlessly in the breaking dawn, by the old well house, and waited for Seth's latest revelation.

"Libby smelled printer's ink in Olson's boarding house, and we've got to know why, right?"

They nodded.

"Yesterday we got most of the kids in the wards organized for night patrols, right?"

Again they nodded.

"Libby, your birthday's on Thursday, right?"

"Now wait a minute," she said nervously, "I don't think I like the sound of this."

Seth stopped in his tracks. "Why not?"

"You're talking about my birthday. That's why."

"Right! The reason is, you're going to have a birthday party, and at the party we're going to have the biggest scavenger hunt ever."

Libby's face puckered. "Scavenger hunt? You can't. That'll ruin everything!"

"Ruin what," Seth replied.

"My party. I've got it all planned. Just a few friends for dinner, and a cake, and some dancing and singing. You can just forget about making my birthday party into a scavenger hunt." Her lower lip protruded defiantly.

"Aw Libby, come on. The Prophet asked us to do this."

"The Prophet asked you to ruin my birthday party with a scavenger hunt? Well, we'll see about that! I'll just go ask him." She bobbed her head dramatically for effect.

Seth's head dropped forward in resignation. "All right, the Prophet didn't ask us to have a scavenger hunt. But he did ask us to help find those counterfeiters, and to do that we've got to know if that man up in Olson's boarding house is printing stuff in his room. And the only way I can figure to get into that room is go on a scavenger hunt!"

Abe look puzzled. "A scavenger hunt in Olson's boarding house?"

"Aw, come on, Abe," Seth groaned. " Think. When we make the lists of stuff the kids are supposed to get, we'll write down things like orange printer's ink, or old bottles or tubes or whatever they come in, and green too. Maybe trimmings from printed stuff, where they cut the edges straight. Stuff like that. We five will be one of the teams, and we'll just happen to go to Olson's with our list. Anybody got a better idea? We can't just go up there and break into that room some afternoon. That's against the law."

Libby began to pout. "No dinner. No dancing. No

cake. No birthday party. Just a big, dumb, stupid scavenger hunt."

Seth sighed. "Okay okay. Bad idea. No scavenger hunt. I'll think of something else. But it won't be as good as a scavenger hunt."

"You mean it? You'll cancel the scavenger hunt just for me?"

Seth nodded glumly.

"Oh." Libby brightened. "Okay. Well, maybe we should have the scavenger hunt after all. I can have my real party next year. Did you make the lists of stuff to scavenge?"

Seth's mouth dropped open.

Jacob turned to Abe and jerked a thumb towards Libby. "She's nuts."

Libby smiled demurely and ignored them. "Well, do you have the lists?"

"Uh, no," Seth said, "I thought we'd each make a list today and we'll look at them tonight before we meet all the evening patrol kids. We'll agree on five final lists and I'll have them written up for tomorrow night. We'll put the word out about the party tonight, and we got to figure out refreshments and all that stuff, too."

Seth paused and looked at Libby. "I forgot about your parents. Will they object to this?"

Libby reflected for a moment. "I'll take care of that. And maybe the refreshments, too."

Seth saw the gleam in Libby's eye and knew when to stop. "Okay. You all know what we're doing. Get your lists ready for tonight and we'll meet at the Ward at seven o'clock, and the rest of the evening patrol kids come at 7:30."

At 5:30 Libby put down her pencil, scanned her list, and washed for supper. She bowed her head while her father pronounced the blessing on the food, and then she plumped a spoonful of mashed potatoes on her plate and pushed a pocket in the center of the pile. "Please pass the gravy." She poured pungent, brown, steaming gravy into the pocket, and placed the silver ladle back in the bowl.

"I'm so glad about my party. Just a few friends - it will be so nice."

Maude Taylor glanced sideways at her daughter, the last of her four children, and the only one remaining at home. Middle aged, wisened to the ways of children by her first three, Maude had long since recognized the genius in Libby. She interfered in Libby's schemes only when she saw they were dangerous or harmful to someone, and that was very, very seldom. Inside, Maude marvelled at how many people danced to Libby's tunes, without ever knowing there was music, or if they did, who was orchestrating it.

She's going to change her party plans. I know it as sure as I'm sitting here. Maude continued with her supper, listening.

"That's nice, dear," Benjamin Taylor said, without looking up from his newspaper. "Say, this is quite an editorial you kids wrote."

"I'm glad I said no to the kids."

"That's nice, dear," he said again, then stopped. "What kids?"

"The kids from the other wards."

"No about what?"

"My birthday party."

"What did you say no to?"

"Well, they wanted to come."

"Just like that? Invited themselves?"

"Not exactly."

Benjamin put his fork down and leaned back in his chair. "You better tell me about all this."

Maude cut a small piece of veal roast and chewed slowly while she watched.

"There's nothing to tell. We got them all organized

yesterday for the evening patrols, like in the newspaper editorial, and they were real excited, and one of them said, oh, we've just got to have a party, and they all said great idea, it's Libby's birthday next week, let's have a birthday party for her."

She stopped and stared at her plate. "I said no."

Benjamin pursed his mouth for a moment in thought. "You mean the kids in town wanted to put on a party for you?"

"Sort of."

"What's 'sort of'?"

"They said, let's have a big scavenger hunt. Can you think of anything more dumb than a scavenger hunt for a birthday party?"

Benjamin shrugged. "I don't know, sounds sort of fun. Maybe the kids need something like that right now. It would bring the whole town together now that the spring plowing and planting are done."

Maude shook her head slightly. She's going to have a scavenger hunt. Why?

"Oh, daddy, you can't mean that. Why, the house wouldn't hold them all. And we'd have to have . . . we could never bake a birthday cake big enough."

"Their parents know about this?"

Libby looked thoughtful. "I suppose so."

"That's a lot of votes," he murmured. His head dropped forward and for several seconds he stared at his plate in deep concentration.

"I think it's a pretty good idea. Tell you what. You let the kids have their scavenger hunt, and I'll open City Hall for the crowd. We'll order a dozen big cakes and we'll freeze twenty gallons of ice cream, and throw a party the kids won't soon forget, in honor of the youth patrols, and your birthday. What do you say?"

"Oh, daddy!" Libby said with huge eyes. "That isn't what I had in mind for my birthday at all!"

Benjamin continued paternally. "I know, I know, but there are times when you've got to put aside your own wishes for the good of others, and the more I think on this the more I think this is one of those occasions. We haven't got much time to waste. Yes or no."

Libby sat back in her chair and looked humble. "For the good of all?"

"Yes, young lady, for the good of all."

"Is it the Christian thing to do?"

"It is the Christian thing to do."

"Then for the good of all, I'll do it."

Maude closed her eyes and silently, gently, shook her head, as she had so many times, and neither Benjamin nor Libby noticed.

Libby glanced at the tall, carved grandfather clock standing in the corner of the dining room. "OH! I nearly forgot! I've got to get ready for our first evening patrol. I'm supposed to be at the Ward in forty minutes."

"You kids be careful," Benjamin warned, "and stay together. Don't do anything foolish." He watched her skip up the stairs.

"I promise," she answered over her shoulder.

She changed to her high topped shoes and a work dress, and tied her long hair back with a bow, modeled before the mirror for a moment, grabbed her list, and trotted outside. Seth, Abe, Jacob and Hawk were waiting at the ward.

"Got your list?," Seth asked.

Libby handed it to him and he compared it with the other four.

"Hey, this is great!" He turned to Libby and said, nervously, "How about your parents?"

Libby tossed her head. "Daddy's going to open City Hall for the scavenger hunt, and he's going to have a dozen big cakes and twenty gallons of ice cream."

Seth's mouth fell open. "He is?"

"Well of course he is," Libby said, and tossed her head again, as though it were an every day thing.

Abe's cheeks ballooned as he exhaled. "How did you do that?"

Jacob shook his head. "Don't ask."

Hawk smiled.

Others began to arrive and by seven thirty, more than one hundred young people had gathered, excited, chattering, impatient. Seth climbed to the fourth step on the big, cement stairs leading up to the double front doors of the church, and turned to face the crowd.

"Welcome welcome welcome," he called. Tonight we start our Youth Patrol project. You're all organized and you know what part of town you're responsible for. I don't need to take time telling you what to do."

Applause broke out and Seth raised his hands for quiet.

"There is another announcement. Libby Taylor will make it."

Libby walked up beside Seth, and when she announced the scavenger hunt and birthday party, with cake and ice cream, the shout was deafening.

Seth waited until it had quieted. "Report back here at ten o'clock. Remember, anything looks wrong, get word to your local high councilman. Be careful. God bless you."

Sunset yielded to dusk, and dusk to dark, as the groups walked the streets of the town, each in their neighborhood. At ten o'clock they gathered back at the ward building and once again Seth settled them.

"You leaders, anything to report?"

"Yes," called Addie Stewart. "We saw two men walking towards town. They walked in the shadows and looked suspicious, and I'm sure one of them was drunk. We tried to talk to them but they cursed at us and we ran."

Seth perked up. "Where?"

"Over on second east."

"Did you get a look at them?"

"One was really husky, and the other one, the drunk one, was slender."

"Anybody else see them," he exclaimed?

"Yeah, we did," Bobby Perkins said.

"Where?"

"Going right into town, not far from Eagle monument."

"Same description?"

"Yep. One like a bull, one skinny, sort of staggering."

"Did you report it to the High Council?"

"Sure did.

"Great! That's real progress. I'll make a record of it and turn it in to the police in the morning. We go again Wednesday night, and Thursday we have the scavenger hunt. You did great tonight. Head for home. And thanks."

The groups left, chattering and talking, while the Brigade stayed behind.

"Hawk," Seth said, "did those two sound like the ones you saw that night at the hotel?"

Hawk nodded.

"Headed towards town, and it sounds like they could have been coming from Olson's boarding house, where that third man stays."

"The mystery man," Libby said.

"Okay," Seth said, "we'll see. Hawk, Wednesday the rest of us will cover our neighborhood, but you go on up to Eagle monument and watch for those two. Okay?"

Wednesday the air was dry and the sun hot, and there was no wind. By evening the dead air in the high mountain valley was stifling. A welcome breeze drifted down from City Creek Canyon and Emigration Canyon with the setting of the sun, to cool the valley for the night.

The patrols met and scattered, and just before ten o'clock Seth was at the ward building, waiting for the last of them to return and report. He turned to Jacob and Libby and Abe, face drawn in concern.

"Seen Hawk?"

Jacob shook his head.

"No," Libby said, "and I'm worried."

Seth climbed the steps. "Leaders, anything to report?"

The leaders shook their heads.

"How about those two from Monday? The heavy guy and the skinny guy? Anybody see them?"

Addie shook her head. "We looked really good, but we didn't see them."

Bobby Perkins chimed in, "Neither did we. Maybe they left town."

"Okay. Thanks. Be sure to be at City Hall at six o'clock tomorrow night for the party. Scavenger hunt starts at 6:15 and ends sharp at 8:15. Then prizes for the winners, and cake and ice cream for everyone."

Seth waited for the groups to disperse, then turned to Jacob, deep concern showing in his face. "Walk Libby home. I'm going to find Hawk."

Jacob shook his head. "If you're going, we're all going."

The four of them trotted north, working their way towards town, and stopped on South Temple and First East. Across the street they could see the great carved eagle, resting atop the graceful, curved supports, by the Beehive House.

Seth glanced up and down South Temple, towards the Lion House, and temple square.

"Let's go to Hawk's place. Maybe he's there."

Abe pointed. "Nope. He's right over there."

From the shadows of Eagle monument, Hawk materialized and crossed the street like a shadow. He stopped facing Seth. "I found them and tracked them. They're up there on Whisky Street." Seth looked at Jacob and Jacob looked at Libby, and then Abe.

Whisky Street! The name given East Temple, also known as Main Street, by riff raff who lived for drink and cards and second floor rooms and gambling. There was fighting every night, and killings at least once each week. Whisky Street was a heartbreaking sorrow to Brigham Young and the saints who had walked two thousand miles to be rid of sin and corruption, only to have it thrust upon them once again, by the army of the United States of America, right in the heart of their dream of Zion.

James Buchanan, President of the United States, had listened to W. W. Drummond, an evil and designing man, and believed the Mormons were living as savages in the far reaches of the unwanted, barren wilderness, and had conspired against the United States. He declared it his duty to put down their rebellion.

He ordered Colonel Albert Sidney Johnston to march an army of 2,500 United States soldiers from Fort Leavenworth to that mountain valley, there to crush the rebellion and restore peace and morality to the degenerate and murderous Mormons.

Reports of the army reached Brigham Young before they had come one hundred miles. He called in Lot Smith.

"Slow the incoming army, stop them if you can, but Brother Smith, do not take one human life. Porter will help."

The two of them, with a handful of other young, courageous volunteers, found the incoming army on the plains. They burned Fort Bridger, which the Mormons had bought from Jim Bridger, and then Fort Supply, which they owned, and left no supplies for the invaders. They burned the grass so there was no graze left for the army livestock, and ran off their horses and mules, and used a buffalo rifle to shoot holes in their cooking pots while they prepared their suppers. They stampeded buffalo through their camps, fouled the water holes, set up fake ambushes in the canyons, and delayed the army for months, giving Brigham the time he needed to prepare the saints.

Colonel Johnston marched his army into Salt Lake City, only to find it deserted, with tumbleweeds jammed against every building, ready for the torch that would burn the city to the ground if Colonel Johnston and his army tried to occupy it.

Wisely, Colonel Johnston marched on through, south past the Point of the Mountain, to the west side of Utah Lake, where he set up his permanent Camp, and named it Camp Floyd.

Inevitably, as it has been from the time armies have marched, a town sprang up near the camp, filled with gambling, alcohol, and painted, foolish women who lived on the pay received by the soldiers. The town was named Fairfield. It became known as Frog Town, and sometimes, Dobie, but by whatever name, it was a quagmire of evil.

The decadent evils of Fairfield soon found their way to Salt Lake City. First one business on First East Street began to sell drink to the soldiers, then another, then one opened a card table, and then rooms opened on the second floor and women came.

"Close it down," Brigham thundered.

"You will obey the laws of the United States," Colonel Johnston retorted, "and those businesses will remain open."

The moral decay thrived, within the very shadow of the holy temple of the lord, and Brigham bowed his head and wept for his dream of Zion, and his beloved saints, but there was nothing he could do to close down the evil influences of Whisky Street.

Years later, General Johnston sensed that the stories

heard by President Buchanan were false. He carefully wrote a detailed report, stating the saints were good, God fearing people, and loyal citizens of the United States. He sent the report east, and in time, President Buchanan received it, and confirmed the truth of it.

President Buchanan regretted his monumental error in believing evil men, and sending an army to put down a rebellion that never existed. His folly was blazed across the front page of the nation's newspapers, and it came to be known as "Buchanan's Blunder." President Buchanan never recovered from it. He finally commissioned Colonel Johnston a Brigadier General and ordered him to return with the army, and Camp Floyd was deserted.

Fairfield, or Frog Town, continued, as did the dens of sin on East Temple, or Main Street, kept alive by the increasing arrival of people into the valley who did not belong to the church, nor who shared the priceless spiritual values of the saints.

But in the meantime, the Saints had to live with the unwanted blight of Camp Floyd, Fairfield, and Whisky Street.

Seth drew a sharp breath. "Whisky street? They're up there?"

"Yes," Hawk said and pointed to a saloon where a honky-tonk piano banged and raucous laughter could be heard through the swinging doors, and lights were on in the second floor windows. "They went into that place, called the Oasis about an hour ago and haven't come out. At least not the front."

Seth hesitated and blew a long breath. "Wheewww."

"You thinking of going up there," Hawk asked quietly.

"We been looking for those two for weeks. We never been this close."

"People get killed up there."

"I know."

Seth squared his shoulders. "I'm going to take a look.

You go on home."

"Not likely," Hawk said. "Let's go. I know the alley behind those saloons."

Hawk led Seth over to First West Street, and came to the mouth of the alley from the dark side of the street.

Lights burned in the second floor windows along the back of the buildings and cast bizarre shadows. Curtains stirred in open windows and harsh laughter and an occasional loud curse of both men and women reached them. A door opened and light flooded the alley for a moment while a big man wearing a bartenders' apron threw a small man sprawling in the dirt. The small man tried to rise, then collapsed, unconscious.

Hawk motioned Seth to follow, and darted up the alley to crouch behind a barrell and a smashed shipping crate. He pointed and said softly, "The Oasis is right up there, two doors."

"What do we do when we get there," Seth whispered.

"Maybe we try to sneak in."

Hawk waited a moment until he was certain the drunk man was not going to move, then sprinted further and crouched behind a dozen empty whiskey boxes, Seth right behind.

"Right over there," Hawk said. "The back door."

Two windows on the second floor, above the door, were open and lighted. From one came loud sounds of a man and a woman talking, arguing about whisky. There was no sound from the other.

"I'll go first," Hawk said, and moved swiftly to flatten himself against the wall beside the door. Above the door, a broken sign with the word "OASIS" hung on one nail.

Seth waited until Hawk nodded, and started his dash across the expanse of the alley. He had taken three running steps when the back door began to open. He hit the wall when the door was fully opened, and he flattened himself beside Hawk as a drunk man staggered out and fell to his knees, followed by another man who cursed and jerked the door closed. The men were not five feet from the boys, who stood frozen with their backs against the rough boards.

In the three seconds of light from the door, both Hawk and Seth had seen the two men clearly. The man now on his knees was a slender man with a large, red nose. The man now standing over him was shorter, thick shouldered, thick necked.

And neither man had seen the boys!

"Stupid!," the blocky man spat. "Drunk and shootin' off your mouth in there for everybody to hear! We'll have the law on us and be in prison!"

The drunk man tried to rise. "I didn't say nothin'. Nothin', I swear."

"Nothin'! Only where we done it! Enough to get us convicted."

The thick man's hand dropped to his right side and whipped up and Seth caught his breath. In the shadowy light he saw the flash of the raised knife blade.

"I ought to . . ."

"No, no, you got no cause . . don't do it . ."

The swarthy man's face was suddenly a mask of evil, and the raised hand flashed down and Hawk and Seth heard the soft sound of the knife driving home. The man on the ground grunted and a whining sound came from his throat as the knife struck, once, twice, three times in his back, and he sank onto his stomach and his legs moved, and then he was still.

The thick man wiped the knife blade on the leg of the body at his feet and thrust it back in its sheath.

"That ought to stop your loose tongue," he muttered, and a wicked chuckle rolled from his throat. He looked quickly up and down the alley, then spun on his heel to go back into the back door of the saloon, and stopped still. He was facing both boys, less than six feet from them. Seth could see the outline of the square face, but not the detail. For a moment the three of them stood transfixed in shock and surprise, and then Seth grabbed Hawk's shoulder.

"RUN!", he shouted, and the boys pivoted to their left and sprinted up the alley as though the Devil were after them. The thick man shouted "STOP" and ran after them for twenty feet before he realized he would never catch them, and he stopped and ran back to the saloon door.

Seth sprinted to the end of the alley, across South Temple, then east to the Lion House wall. He was over the wall in two seconds, between the carriage house, and Brigham's prize rose garden and compost pile. Hawk was right behind him, and he slowed as he whistled the mourning dove signal, and then he stopped and waited.

From the dark door at the back of the Lion House, a shadow appeared and walked to him.

"Who's there," came the twangy voice.

"Seth Dunn," Seth whispered hoarsely. "Hawk and I were over in the alley behind the Oasis. Remember the two men I told you about, the heavy man and the skinny one? The heavy man killed the skinny one."

Porter's head jerked forward. "You two was at the Oasis?"

Seth plunged on, his voice high and breathless. "Just now, and we saw . . ."

Porter cut him off. "Thunderation!," he exclaimed. "Don't you know there's people in there that would cut your throat just to get your shoes? What were you using for good sense, going there?"

Seth's shoulders sagged. "I know it was wrong, but we saw a murder."

"Wait here,"

Porter ran to the house and returned in a moment with his pistols buckled around his waist. "Take me where you saw it."

Three minutes later Hawk and Seth slowed as they approached the door in the alley, and the stopped in surprised amazement. There was no body, no blood, no signs of a struggle. Nothing. They stood staring, incredulous.

"Right here," Seth said and pointed. "With a knife, right here. Hawk and I were against that wall, not six feet away."

Quickly Porter looked behind the whiskey boxes and then the barrel and shipping crate near by, then trotted to the rear door of the Oasis and grasped the handle.

Locked.

He stepped back one step, draw both pistols at the same time, cocked them, raised his right foot and kicked hard. The door jamb splintered and the door swung inward, and light and the sounds of raucous cursing and the tinny piano flooded outward.

Porter marched in, arms extended, cocked pistols covering everyone in the back section of the saloon. He continued to the end of the bar and every man and every woman in the place watched his every move. They could make no mistake about the long hair, nor the eyes that glowed like embers, nor the muzzles of two cocked Colt .44 pistols. They knew they were facing Orrin Porter Rockwell. No one moved and no one spoke in the dead silence that enveloped the room.

Quietly Seth and Hawk slipped through the back door and stood by the back wall, unnoticed, nearly hypnotized by what they were watching.

"I'm going to ask just once," Porter said. "Where's the man who just committed murder in the alley?"

No one spoke.

"Everybody in this room, drop your gunbelts and shuck your knives. You got ten seconds."

Trembling fingers opened belt buckles, and holstered guns and sheathed knives tumbled to the floor.

"Aw come on, Porter," the bartender started. "We'd tell you if we knew, but we don't."

"Yeah, he's right," said a man sitting at a card table.

"What'd he look like," asked a painted woman. "We never saw nothin'."

"Thick shoulders, thick neck," Porter growled. "Dark."

"Sure. I know who you mean," the bartender volunteered. "He was in here with a friend drinkin' half the evening. But they left maybe fifteen minutes ago and we ain't seen 'em since. The skinny one was drunk. Probably fell down out there in the alley and the big guy left him to sleep it off, and it only looked like a killin'."

"Yeah, that's what likely happened," said another man standing at the bar.

"No, there was a killin'," Porter hissed. "And it's likely the killer hauled the body in here to hide it, and hisself."

"Nossir," the bartender said emphatically, "nobody hauled no dead body in here tonight. I swear it. You kin take this place apart, upstairs too, and you aint goin' to find no body and no murderer. I swear it. Go look for yerself."

Porter locked eyes with the bartender for a moment.

"I reckon if he did bring the body in here, he's gone with it by now. No matter. I'm closin' this place down for the night and I'm going to take a look. Barkeep, start turning down them lamps and the rest of you, pick up yer gunbelts with yer left hands, and get outta here. Women too. Start now."

"Now wait a minute," the bartender said defiantly. "You can't just walk in here and accuse us of coverin' up a murder and order us to . . ."

Porter slanted his right pistol and the first shot blasted and the big lamp behind the bar shattered.

"You hard of hearin'?," he rasped at the bartender. "I said shut 'er down. Douse them lamps or I'll do it for you."

The stampede nearly took the front swinging doors off their hinges as men and women alike stormed out onto South Temple and scattered. Thirty seconds later the Oasis was dark, save for one lamp that Porter carried as he opened every door on the second floor with his pistol drawn, searched every room, then returned downstairs while the bartender locked and barred the front door. The bartender followed Porter to the back door, closed it when Porter was outside, and stacked whisky boxes against it to prop it shut because the jamb had been splintered by Porter's entrance. Seth and Hawk had long since slipped outside and were pressed against the wall outside, waiting, and the three walked back up the alley.

"Don't you kids never ever do anything like that again. You understand?"

"Yes sir. I feel bad, real bad, that it turned out that way."

"I'll go tell the constable," Porter said, "and they'll come investigate. I'll take my own look at first light in the morning, but I'll tell you right now, they won't find anything and neither will I."

They crossed the street and angled north.

"Maybe some good can come of all this," Porter said. "If you was that close, did you hear anything?"

"Only that they had argued about something. The heavy one said the skinny one had got drunk and talked too much, and that he had told people 'where they done it.' I don't know what he meant, but he said it was enough to get them convicted."

"Convicted?" Porter reflected a moment. "You kids are getting close. If that heavy man would kill his partner, he sure wouldn't have any trouble killing one of you if he figures this thing out."

Seth slowed and Porter looked back at him. "What's the matter?"

"He saw us out in that alley. It wasn't very light, but we were face to face, five feet apart. And he knows we saw the murder."

"It's time for you kids to get out of this," Porter said with finality. "Remember Brigham's orders?"

"Not yet, Porter, please," Seth argued. "We're so close to solving this whole thing. We saw his face, but we couldn't see the details, and if we couldn't see him that clearly, he couldn't see us well enough to identify us. All he knows is there were two people there, and they ran. He doesn't know what we look like."

"He's right," Hawk said. "He doesn't know who we are."

Porter continued walking in silent thought. "Okay. Just a few more days. But I don't like it. Not at all. And don't you ever do anything again like going up to the Oasis at night."

They paused at the Lion House gate.

"We got a couple of problems," Porter said. "First, you two can't tell anyone about this. Word gets out, that killer's going to find out it was kids and then none of your evening patrols will be safe. So don't tell any of the patrols."

"I got to tell the others in the Brigade," Seth replied.

"Swear them to secrecy."

"I will. What's the second thing?"

"Somewhere there's a body. If we can find it, maybe we can arrest that killer for murder and be rid of this whole thing."

Seth nodded. "I won't tell them about the murder, but I'll tell them if they see anyone that looks like that man, go get some of the others as fast as they can. There's safety in numbers."

"Okay," Porter said. "Now you two get on home."

"Thanks, Porter, for your help.," Seth replied, and the boys trotted away in the darkness.

Seven

LIBBY CLAPPED THE FLATS of both hands against the sides of her face and gasped, "You saw a what?"

"A murder!" Seth's eyes were large in the early dawn gray, where the Brigade was standing beside the well-house at the old ward building.

Abe's head jerked forward. "Where? When? Who?"

For five minutes the Brigade stood spellbound in disbelief while Seth and Hawk filled in the details.

"So Porter says we've go two problems. We can't tell anybody because the killer might figure out it was kids, and none of our evening patrols would be safe after that. We'll tell the patrols that if they see anybody like this guy, go find other patrols quick because there's safety in numbers."

He paused for a second. "And the other problem is, there's a body somewhere, and if we could find it, it might be enough to get this guy arrested for murder, and that would probably take care of this whole thing."

"He's probably buried it by now," Jacob said. "If he did, nobody'll find it."

Hawk shook his head. "Maybe. Depends on if he left a trail somewhere."

Seth began to pace, and the others settled back.

He stopped and pulled his upper lip.

"He didn't have much time to hide it, maybe twenty minutes while Hawk and I got Porter and Porter closed down the Oasis. So, if you were that guy, and had killed somebody, and knew you had been seen, and had to hide a body quick, where would you hide it that no one would ever suspect?"

Silence gripped them for several seconds before Jacob broke in. "How about Temple square, right up the block, where all that construction work is going on."

Seth jabbed his finger at the sky. "Exactly! Nobody would look for a dead body on Temple square."

He turned to Hawk. "You live there. You know that place like a book. Can you take a look?"

"Yeah, but I better get going. I need to get there before everybody walks over whatever tracks he left. There's one more problem."

"What's that?"

"He could have put the body somewhere until things quieted down last night and then moved it somewhere. Maybe out on the desert and buried it."

"Yes, I thought of that. But you should go take a look anyway. Report back here at 5:30 this afternoon, before the scavenger hunt. Get going."

Hawk spun and ran.

"Let's get on home," Seth concluded, "but be here to meet Hawk at 5:30, and see what we got by then. Okay?"

Seth worked through his morning chores, and hilled and hoed the corn, then weeded the tomato patch. He stopped from time time to stare vacantly at the hoe, or the clods at his feet, while in his mind he was seeing a knife flash in the shadowy alley, and hearing the sounds in a man's throat as he died. It seemed like some horrible dream, from which he would suddenly awaken.

At the noon meal his mother said, "Seth, you haven't been acting right, out there in the garden. Are you sick?"

"A little."

"Need to lay down?"

"No. It'll pass. I'm okay."

At five o'clock he changed clothes and trotted to the ward building and a few minutes later the rest of the Brigade arrived.

"Hawk, did you find anything," Seth asked anxiously.

Hawk shook his head. "I know that man's tracks, and they weren't there. I've watched and listened today, and nothing happened. If he buried or hid the body there, there's no trace of how he did it."

Doubt crept into Seth's voice. "If he didn't put it there, then where did he put it?"

"Moved it afterwards, out in the desert somewhere," Jacob volunteered.

"Yeah, I guess you're right. Well, keep an eye open. Come on, we got to get out front. The kids are gathering for the scavenger hunt."

A cheer arose from a hundred young voices when Seth and the others walked around the corner of the ward house. Seth mounted the front steps.

"One announcement first. If you see a suspicious man lurking about while you're on evening patrol in the next few days, go find another patrol quick and stay with them, and send someone to get me. This man might be dangerous, and there is safety in numbers. He's thick in the shoulders and neck. Watch for him."

Silence gripped the group, and then a buzz started among them.

Seth raised his hands. "Enough business. Are you ready for the biggest scavenger hunt ever, and for birthday cake and ice cream afterwards for Libby?"

Applause and cheers filled the air.

"Okay, here's the lists. Be at the City Hall at 8:15 sharp. If you're late, you're disqualified from the prizes."

"What are the prizes," a voice called.

"Homemade pulled taffy, by the Relief Society."

Cheers again filled the air, with the thought of sweet, chewy taffy. Quickly the team captains stepped forward to receive their lists, and then read them aloud to the teams amid a torrent of laughter and questions.

"What's a daguerreotype?," cried a girls voice.

"A picture of your grandpa," answered another.

"Who's got an odometer?," called another.

"What is an odometer?"

"That's a book about odors, dummy," came the answer.

Seth smiled and the Brigade watched the groups scatter in every direction.

"Okay, come on," he said.

They stopped first at Fulton's, and then at Kelsey's, and then Seth slowed and took a deep breath.

"Okay, here we go. Next stop is Olson's boarding house. We got to get into that upstairs corner room, but it's got to look normal. Be careful what you say."

Their steps sounded hollow on the front porch, and Seth knocked.

"Seth," sister Olson said through the screen door. "What brings you kids here?"

"Have you finished supper with your boarders? We don't want to interfere."

"Oh yes. They're finished."

"It's Libby's birthday," Seth continued excitedly, "and we're having the scavenger hunt."

"Oh yes," Sigrid Olson exclaimed. "I remember. How can I help?"

"Great," Seth said. "Well, let's see." He ran a finger

down their list. "Have you got a buttonhook? We'll bring it back, I promise."

"I think so. Come on in."

She swung the screen door open and they walked into the parlor. A few of the boarders sat in chairs, reading, two playing dominoes. They nodded a greeting to the Brigade.

In a moment Sister Olson reappeared from the long hallway and handed the buttonhook to Libby. Libby eyed the boarders, who had turned their attention to the Brigade and sister Olson.

"Anything else?," sister Olson asked.

"How about an old powder horn?"

"Oh mercy, no. I don't keep guns on the place. They scare me."

An elderly border put down a domino and said, "By cracky, I think I still got one. Up in my room. Give me a minute."

"Oh," cried Libby, "how nice of you."

"What else," asked sister Olson, as the bent old man hobbled down the hall.

"How about an apple corer?"

In a moment she returned from the kitchen and handed it to Libby, as the old man returned with a battered old powder horn. The shoulder strap was worn, and the leather bindings were patched. The old man handed it to Jacob.

"There. Will you bring it back, sonny?," he asked.

"Sure will."

"That old horn has been with me fifty years in these mountains," the old man said wistfully. "If she could talk, she'd tell many a tale. I'd hate to lose her now."

Carefully Jacob wound the shoulder strap around the old horn. "I'll bring it back just like it is, I promise."

A smile crossed the wrinkled old face. "Good." Seth

continued running his finger down the sheet. "How about an old engraving? Any kind."

Sister Olson shook her head. "No, I don't have one."

Libby turned to the other boarders. "Would any of you happen to have one? I would surely appreciate it."

"How about that young fellow on the second floor." A small, prim, gray haired little lady, reading next to a window, looked over the tops of her glasses. "Seems to me I've seen him with some things that looked like they were printed from an engraving."

Seth glanced at Libby.

"OH!", Libby exclaimed. "Is he up there now?"

Sister Olson thought for a moment. "I didn't see him leave after supper."

"Would you let us go up and ask," Libby pleaded.

Sister Olson shrugged. "Sure. It's all in fun."

"What's his name," Libby asked as she started for the stairs.

"John Jones."

"I can remember that. Do you want to come up with us?"

"You go ahead," Sister Olson said. "I've got supper dishes to do. Just say I said it was all right."

The Brigade mounted the stairs and hurried to the corner room and Seth paused for a moment before he rapped on the door, and he whispered, "Be careful what you say."

He rapped on the door.

There was no answer.

He rapped again, a little harder, then put his ear to the door and listened. Faint scurrying sounds came from inside. Seth raised his hand to knock again when a voice came through the door.

"Who's there?"

Libby spoke up. "A group of kids from town on a scavenger hunt. Sister Olson said it was all right."

The door opened a few inches and a face appeared in the crack. "What do you want?," the man growled suspiciously.

Libby smiled her humble smile. "We're here on a scavenger hunt and we need to get . . ."

"Not interested," said the man and slammed the door.

"Well," Libby huffed as she jammed her hands on her hips. "That was rude."

Seth led the way back to the parlor.

"The man wasn't interested," he said to Sister Olson. "Anyway, thanks for the things we got. We'll return them tomorrow."

The Brigade hurried out the front door and they walked to the corner, where Libby stopped them.

"Did you smell it?," she asked.

"Smell what," Abe asked.

"The printer's ink when he opened the door."

"No."

"Well, it was there, just like Brother Dudley's print shop. He's printing something inside that room. We've got to get inside somehow."

"How," Jacob asked. "Break in?"

"No, of course not," Seth said, and began to pace. Suddenly he stopped and pulled at his upper lip.

"When does she clean those rooms each day? You know, dust and change the bedding?"

"Every morning around ten," Hawk said. "She opens the windows and hangs some of the bedding out to air it, and the room, while she does the rest of the work. I saw her twice when I was looking for tracks. She doesn't take but about five minutes on each room."

Libby brightened. "Then maybe there's a way."

Seth looked at her with a quizzical eye. "Can you handle it?"

"How,?" Jacob exclaimed.

"Oh, you'll see," Libby said teasingly. "Ask me

tomorrow when we go on patrol." They continued to the Forsgren's place with their list for the scavenger hunt, and got a pewter cup with a broken handle, and to the Dennis place and got a harness buckle, before Hawk glanced at the Oquirrh mountains west of the Salt Lake. The sun had set half an hour earlier, leaving a border of gold resting on the purple line of the earth.

"Better start back," Hawk said. "Getting late."

They quickly made their way to the City Hall, where most of the teams were gathered on the grass, chattering, laughing, comparing lists and things they had gotten from all over the valley. Long tables stood in rows, with colored bunting draped and a great banner that said "HAPPY BIRTHDAY LIBBY."

"Okay," Seth announced, "team leaders come on over to this table and bring your lists and the things you got."

Half an hour later all the lists had been checked against the items called for, and re-checked by all the team leaders. They were in agreement.

Seth climbed onto a table. "The winner is," Seth said, "Addie's team."

Addie squealed, "OH NO" and everyone clapped while she blushed.

"And here's the prize!" Seth announced and held up a large box. "Ten pounds of homemade taffy for the team to divide."

There was a great round of applause.

"And for all of the rest of us, we've got a smaller package of taffy for each of us in the boxes on the tables. Honor system. Take one piece."

There was a rush and the taffy disappeared in seconds.

"And now for the big event. We all sing Happy Birthday for Libby."

They sang it twice while Libby beamed.

Seth looked at Benjamin Taylor and Benjamin nodded and Seth faced the crowd once more. "Hold your places for five minutes, and our good Mayor, Brother Taylor, will have the cake and ice cream set up on the tables, and you can eat your fill."

A great shout arose and chatter continued while the cakes were delivered and cut, and the wet burlap was unwound from the ice cream churns, and bowls and plates and forks and spoons were set out.

"Bishop Lundgren will offer the blessing," Seth announced.

Bishop Lundgren bowed his head and thanked their Lord for their bounteous blessings, and the wonderful occasion that brought them together, and he blessed the refreshments.

"Amen," he said, and all else was lost in the rush to the tables. The ice cream and cake steadily disappeared amid the happy chatter and laughter of the young people. Each wished Libby a happy birthday, and then they all bowed their heads while Heber Knight of the High Council offered a benediction, and thanked the Lord for the good evening they had shared, and for watching over the youth.

"Come on," Seth said after the last of the teams had gone, "let's walk Libby home."

Halfway there, Hawk paused and looked back.

"See something," Seth asked.

"Maybe heard something," Hawk replied as he peered back into the darkness. "Maybe not."

The following morning, Libby was at the corner behind a great cottonwood tree, spying on Sister Olson's boarding house at ten o'clock. She watched as each window was opened, bedding hung over the window sill, and five minutes later pulled back in, and the window to the next room opened. It was nearly 10:30 before the window to the back room on the second floor opened and bedding draped out to catch the morning sunshine.

Libby dashed to the front door and rapped, then

entered, holding a small brown paper bag in her hand. The little lady seated by the window reading, looked over her spectacles.

"Mrs. Olson's upstairs cleaning, missy," she said, smiling. "How was the scavenger hunt?"

"Oh, it was loads of fun. I'll just run up to return the things she gave us."

She skipped up the stairs in a flash and her shoes clicked on the polished hardwood floor as she ran down the hall. The door to room number eight was open and Libby stopped in the doorway.

"Sister Olson," she said, "I hope I'm not intruding. I just wanted to return the buttonhook and the apple corer."

She took them from her dress pocket. "And oh yes, the powder horn that nice little man let us use." She offered the brown paper bag.

"Thank you, Libby," Mrs. Olson said while she worked with a feather duster. "Just put them there on the table."

Libby walked around the bed, to the table next to the window, and carefully put the articles down. Her eyes darted everywhere, saw everything.

Beneath the table was a black satchel, partially open. Inside, barely visible, was a cloth of some sort, and the wooden handles of the tools of an artisan of some kind. The odor of printer's ink was strong.

The closet door stood partially opened, and among the articles of clothing inside was a worn, brown woolen coat.

Libby's mouth became a straight line. I must look inside that satchel, she resolved.

Sister Olson gathered the bedding from the window sill and turned to make the bed.

"Oh," Libby said, "let me help you."

"I can manage this," Mrs. Olson said. "Land, I do it every day, but thank you."

"No, not at all," Libby said. "Let me help you."

While she smoothed the sheets and tucked them in, and then the blankets and finally the thick comforter, Libby asked, "Do you hang the bedding out every day?"

"Most good days, yes. Good sunshine makes it stay fresh longer."

They finished and Mrs. Olson looked around the room with an air of pride. "Well, that's the last one," she said. "Now I've got to go down and start dinner."

"Oh," Libby exclaimed, "that reminds me. I promised mother I would get your recipe for that berry pie - the most famous pie in the valley. Would you consent to letting mother have it?"

"Why land, child, there's no secret to that. Of course."

Libby followed her down the stairs, then to the kitchen, where Sister Olson pointed to a chair. "Sit down and I'll tell you how to bake those pies."

"Do you have a recipe? Written out, I mean."

Sister Olson pursed her mouth for a moment. "I think so. Let me see where I put it." She opened an orderly cupboard and began looking through a filing basket.

"Oh my," Libby exclaimed. "I think I dropped my pencil upstairs while we were making that bed. I'll run get it. Is the room open?"

"Here's the key," Sister Olson said, and drew the ring from her apron pocket. "Number eight."

Libby ran up the stairs and quickly opened the door. She dashed around the bed and knelt by the table. With trembling hands she opened the top of the satchel and peered inside, and pulled the stained, wadded cloth out, and straightened it, and her eyes suddenly popped wide.

The stains were black, mixed with generous amounts of orange and green.

She looked inside the bag at the many hand tools, tossed in carelessly. Each wooden handle had a steel shank protruding from one end, and each steel shank had a different cutting head, with the smallest of points and sharpened edges Libby had ever seen. A hardwood mallet was laid in one end.

She shoved the cloth back inside as it had been, closed the bag and pushed it back beneath the table, and impulsively pivoted and pulled up the bedclothes to peer under the bed.

A long, low wooden box lay near the head of the bed. She tugged with all her strength, and slowly slid it out until one end was exposed. The box was in two parts, upper and lower. She pried the upper part away and for one brief moment peered inside.

She gasped! Each half of the box contained a plate, each matching the other. Each was beautifully engraved with designs of olive leaves, and flowers. In a divided section at one end were several zinc tubes, empty and rolled up, and two that were partially filled, and capped. The stains around the caps were green and orange. She settled the upper half back into place and swung her feet around to push the entire apparatus back under the bed, where it had been.

"Libby, did you find it?", came Sister Olson's voice up the stairs.

"Just a minute," Libby answered, "I'll be down."

She quickly rose and darted around the foot of the bed and opened the closet door. She jammed her hand in one pocket of the old brown coat, then the other, felt paper, and jerked out a worn envelope, with a letter inside.

"Libby," are you coming?

"Right now, Sister Olson."

She read the name of the sender and the person receiving the letter, and closed her eyes and repeated to herself, "From Myron Brewer to David McKenzie, Brewer to McKenzie, Fairfield to St. Louis."

She jammed the letter back in the pocket and quickly ran to the hallway, closed and locked the door, and ran downstairs. "I'm sorry it took so long, but I couldn't find it anywhere," she said. "I guess I lost it someplace else."

"No matter," Sister Olson said. "I've got one."

Five minutes later Libby laid the pencil down on the shiny, clean oil cloth on Sister Olson's dinner table and looked at the carefully printed recipe.

"Thank you so much. Mother will be thrilled." Libby threw an arm around Sister Olson and hugged her.

"No thanks necessary. Tell Margaret I said hello."

"Tell that little man we appreciated the use of his powder horn." Sister Olson walked Libby to the front door and watched her dart down the stairs and start up the street at a run.

"It isn't seemly for a girl her age to run like that," Sister Olson observed. She shrugged. "'Course she only turned fourteen yesterday. It'll take a week or two, I imagine. This new generation...."

Libby stormed across her front porch, up to her room, grabbed a pencil and quickly wrote on the back of the recipe card, "From Myron Brewer Fairfield to David McKenzie St Louis." She threw the pencil down and dashed back out of the house.

Margaret, bewildered by the whirlwind that had streaked into and out of the house, followed onto the porch, calling after Libby, "What in the world are you doing," but she should have saved her breath.

Libby stopped breathlessly in Seth's cucumber patch, where he was setting the corrugates for water.

"I was there - I saw inside the black satchel," she gasped, as the words came tumbling. "There was a cloth with green and orange, and some tools, and a box with green and orange paint tubes, and some sort of stuff for a printing machine - I saw it, all of it."

"Slow down. Where," Seth said.

Libby tried to control her breathing. "The corner room at Olson's."

"What did the tools look like?"

"Just wood handles with metal things sticking out one

end."

"That has to be engraving equipment," Seth exclaimed.

"And under the bed was a big wooden box with two halves, and each half had a metal plate that was carved."

"Engraved plates! Used for counterfeiting," Seth exclaimed. "That's what they had on the mule that night when Hawk tracked them from the hotel to Olson's place. They moved the printing equipment."

"That isn't all," Libby panted. "There was a letter, from Myron Brewer in Fairfield to David McKenzie in St. Louis. I wrote it down." She thrust the note at Seth.

"David McKenzie? Who's he?"

"I don't know."

Seth paced for a moment. "Of course! He's Jones! John Jones! David McKenzie used a false name at the Olson's."

"Then who's Myron Brewer?"

Seth stroked his chin, then pulled his lip. "I don't know. Did you read the letter?"

"I couldn't. No time."

"We're so close," Seth said, and began pacing. He pulled his lip and stopped.

"You did a great job, Libby. Good work. Go on back home and let me think on this. There are just a few more pieces to this puzzle, and we'll find them."

He watched Libby disappear up the street, and then Seth stopped for a moment to collect his thoughts.

"Porter. I got to see Porter. Tonight."

Eight

SETH STOOD STILL IN THE darkness behind the Lion House wall for several seconds to be certain no one was following before he gave the mourning dove call. Seconds later the twangy voice called quietly, “Who is it?”

“Seth Dunn.”

A moment later Seth was in the shadows inside the wall, facing Porter.

“Libby found the counterfeiting plates and equipment,” he began, and five minutes later concluded, “and that’s what we have as of now.”

“You kids found it?”, Porter said, incredulous.

“Yes.”

“I can’t hardly believe it.”

“Libby described it.”

“David McKenzie?,” Porter muttered to himself.

“Ever heard of him?,” Seth asked.

“Not that I recall. And the other name again?”

“Myron Brewer. He sent the letter from Fairfield to

St. Louis. Libby found it in an old brown coat in McKenzie's closet at Olson's."

"Myron Brewer. Nope, I don't recognize either name."

"It was Hawk that tracked them that night when they moved the equipment from Delmonico's to Olson's. Maybe we should talk with Hawk."

"There was three men that night. We think one of 'em is dead and disappeared. But which one? Brewer?"

Seth shrugged. "Who knows? I think we should talk with Hawk again."

Porter scratched his chin for a minute. "I want to think this whole thing over for a spell, overnight. I got an errand first thing in the morning for Brigham, at the bank. Bring Hawk over around ten. Come to the back wall gate and be sure nobody sees you."

Morning dawned without a cloud in the azure skies and by mid-morning the sun had claimed the day. The clear, dry air had already become oppressive, hot. Seth and Hawk stopped by the four carved columns that swept upward from their cement foundations to support the great, sculpted wooden eagle that spanned the street at the corner of the Beehive House. They paused, and then moved casually to the north end of the wall. They lounged against it for a moment until they were certain no one was watching them, and then they suddenly disappeared. Quickly they darted west to the gate behind the Lion House, and Seth whistled.

Porter guided them into the carriage house, out of sight, just inside the wall.

"Seth tell you what Libby saw?" Porter asked Hawk.

"Yes."

"Figure that's what those three men packed on that mule that night and moved to Olson's?"

"I think it was."

"We got all kinds of fake names floatin' around with those three. Baker, Thomas, Watkins, Jones, and who knows what else. You think the guy at Olson's is David McKenzie, from St. Louis?"

"The letter in his coat is pretty good proof."

"What can you remember about those three from that night they moved the stuff?"

"I remember their tracks, and the skinny one was half drunk. And one of them - the one with the thick neck - wore an army hat."

"You sure about that?"

"Yes. He's the same one that used the knife in the alley behind the Oasis."

Porter suddenly straightened. "Wait a minute. That letter was sent from Fairfield, right down there by Camp Floyd, and you say the thick necked man had on an army hat. Think he might be Brewer, and Brewer might be a soldier boy down at Camp Floyd? He might have mailed the letter from Fairfield because he didn't want nobody at Camp Floyd to know he done it?"

Hawk bobbed his head. "Maybe, maybe not. Brewer might be the dead one."

Porter pursed his mouth. "You're right. We got an engraver and a killer and a dead man that were all partners in a counterfeiting deal, but we don't know if Brewer is the dead partner or the live one."

He paused to draw and release a great breath of air. "I don't like this. We're gettin' too close, but we don't know enough yet to put it all together. We better get the rest of it quick or those two are going to do something rash."

"Maybe we can find out what's in the letter," Seth said.

"Naw," Porter said, "not without breakin' the law. Libby took a hard risk doin' what she did this mornin', and that's enough."

His head dropped forward in deep thought and he walked to the door to the carriage house, staring at the ground, unseeing. Seth followed, Hawk beside him.

Porter stared outside for a long, silent minute.

"I'm going down to Camp Floyd. I got a friend in the Army payroll department. He can tell me if he has someone down there named Myron Brewer on the payroll. It's forty-eight miles, and it'll take two days, and that's a bad worry because if these two smell somethin' wrong they can be long gone in two days."

"Get Abe!" Seth exclaimed.

"For what?"

"He's the best horseman in the valley. He can be down there and back tonight, on Star."

Porter shook his head. "It's 10:30 in the morning. You think someone can cover ninety-six miles and be back here tonight? You're dreamin'."

"No sir," Seth said boldly, "Abe can do it.

"He'll kill the horse."

"Not Star."

"You serious," Porter said in stark disbelief.

Hawk interrupted. "He's serious. Abe and Star can do it."

"I don't believe it. Let me talk with him."

Twenty minutes later Porter faced Abe in the horse barn behind the Rawlins home.

"Seth tells me you can make Fairfield and be back here tonight. I don't believe it."

Abe thought for a minute. "Ninety six miles. Yes, I can be back by midnight."

"You figure to kill the horse?"

"She'll be tired, but she'll be sound."

"Where's this wonder horse?"

Abe stepped to the back of the barn and whistled low, and the gray mare came at a run, and stopped in a cloud of dust with her muzzle a foot from Abe's face.

"There she is," Abe said, and his face glowed with pride. "Short coupled, deep chest, clean legged, intelligent, and she has the endurance that comes in a pure blooded Arabian, and especially in her, more than any horse I know. Once she and I covered twenty eight miles at a hard run to get medicine to save the Ambrose baby."

He turned to face Porter. "If you want something from Fairfield that will help the Prophet, Star and me can have it back here by midnight."

Porter shook his head. "I think I've gone loco! I believe you can do it. Get a pencil and paper. We got a letter to write."

Abe returned from the house in two minutes and Porter handed the paper and pencil to Seth.

"You write what I say."

"If I write it, won't your friend know it isn't from you?"

Porter exhaled and his shoulders slumped. "Nobody much knows this, but - I can't write. Never learned. Joseph was the one that learned to write. I learned the forest, and trackin', and men."

His face reddened and he looked at the ground for a moment, then back at Seth with frank eyes. "Don't be spreadin' that around."

"I won't. What do you want me to write?"

For five minutes Porter dictated, and Seth wrote it, then carefully read it back.

"That's good," Porter said, and turned to Abe.

"Go directly to Colonel Johnston's office and tell his orderly that Porter Rockwell says he needs that answer back here in Salt Lake City by midnight tonight, and it's a matter of life or death. He'll send you to Sergeant-Major Jonas Kinyon in payroll, and he's a friend of mine. Jonas'll give you the answer. Have him write it and sign it and bring it back here to me. Understand?"

"Yes sir."

"Okay. You better leave as soon as you can."

Abe ran to the house and came back with a canteen slung over his shoulder by a strap. He brought Star into the barn, slipped a large, loose leather loop around her neck and vaulted onto her back. He settled his small, wiry frame behind her withers, knees locked gently against her ribs, and pulled the leather loop back.

"Hold on there," Porter said. "Aint you usin' a saddle, or a bridle?"

Abe grinned. "Not with Star. Too much weight for a run like this one. She rides like a rocking horse, and we talk to each other, and I use this loop. That's all she needs."

He clicked his tongue and touched the loop, and the horse spun and trotted out the door into the sunlight.

Porter called, "Take State Street south . . "

Abe cut him off. "No, that wastes four miles. We're headed west, for the Jordan River. There's a trail there that runs to Utah Lake, and we cut south right into Camp Floyd."

"You be careful," Porter called.

"See you before midnight," Abe answered, and he touched the loop and leaned forward and spoke to the mare, and she settled into a steady run with Abe riding loose and easy, as though he and the mare were one.

Porter watched them out of sight before he shook his head. "That boy's one of the finest riders I ever saw. The mare hardly feels him up there."

Abe splashed Star across the Jordan River at a slow, wide, shallow crossing, spoke and nudged, and she turned south onto a trail that was little more than wagon tracks in the grass. Abe raised her to a steady lope with the wind lifting her mane and tail, and sent her forelock flying.

Her driving legs pushed mile after mile behind them, with Abe feeling her breathing and the steady, flawless rhythm of her hooves. An hour after noon he stopped her and rubbed her with dried grass, and let her drink, but not too much, and waited until her breathing became regular. Then he was up onto her willing back again, and he pointed her south on the dim trail, and again settled her into the effortless, relentless run, while he again felt the perfect rhythm of the drive of her hindquarters and the reach and gather of her forelegs.

He passed the narrows at the point of the mountain, angled slightly west with the gentle curve of the Jordan, and stopped once more to rub her with dried grass and let her drink.

"Good girl," he crooned as he gave her time to rest for a few minutes and gather her strength.

Half an hour later he passed a great grove of ancient cottonwoods, skirted the gigantic, old, decaying trunks of half a dozen that had died and been felled by a wind storm a hundred years earlier, and pointed Star's nose due south, towards Camp Floyd.

He slowed for a moment at the sight of half a dozen men not far from the trail, gathered around a low fire, cooking something. They stood and started towards the trail. Their clothing was ragged, their beards long and scraggly, and their mules were badly neglected.

Abe raised Star back to her steady run and passed them as they came running to the trail, cursing at him for not stopping.

Camp Floyd became a black dot in the distance, then a spread of buildings and tents, and then an Army camp. A sentry with a long rifle stopped Abe at the entrance.

"What's your name and business," the soldier demanded.

"Abraham Rawlins. I'm here to see Colonel Johnston. I got a message from Orrin Porter Rockwell."

The soldier blanched. "Let me see it."

Abe pulled it from within his shirt and held it up.

"I'll take it to him," the soldier said gruffly.

"Sorry, sir," Abe said. "I'm to deliver that myself and I have to take an answer back."

"Give me that letter, you young pup," the soldier

demanded, and stepped forward. Abe tugged slightly on the leather loop and Star took four steps backward.

"No sir, this goes to Colonel Johnston, or back to Porter Rockwell. If I take it back, you'll deal with Porter."

The soldier licked dry lips. "Okay. Pass. But you get that delivered and get out of camp."

Abe trotted Star into the camp and looked for the biggest log building he could find. An American flag hung limp from a flagpole at the front of the building, and a sign declared "CAMP FLOYD. COLONEL A. S. JOHNSTON COMMANDING OFFICER."

He dismounted, told Star to stand, and walked onto the boardwalk. The corporal beside the door stopped him.

"Your name and business," please.

"Abraham Rawlins with a message from Orrin Porter Rockwell for Colonel Johnston."

"Show the message."

Abraham showed it.

"Enter," the corporal said, and opened the door for Abe.

Inside an orderly looked at the envelope and rapped on Colonel Johnston's door, and half a minute later Abe was standing in front of a great, scarred desk while Colonel Johnston studied the letter.

The Colonel raised his eyes accusingly. He lit a cigar and raised a cloud of smoke while Abe stood nervously in the silence.

"What's your name again?"

"Abraham Rawlins."

"Porter can't write. Is this a hoax?"

"No sir, he can't. That was written by Seth Dunn. I was there when Porter told him what to write. Those are Porter's words, exact."

"You know Porter personally?" "Yes sir I do."

The Colonel smiled, then grinned. "You're right. He

says Abe Rawlins is pure wheat. Only Porter would say that. How is that old villain?"

"Sir, he's all right. Pure wheat. He said I should tell you he sends his regards."

Colonel Johnston laughed outright, then sat down to write a brief message. He folded it and slipped it inside an envelope from his desk drawer.

"Follow me," he said, and led Abe out onto the boardwalk in front of his headquarters.

"Take this right over to that building," he said, pointing. "Sergeant-Major Jason Kinyon will give you what you need."

He looked at Star. "That your horse?"

"Yes sir."

The Colonel stepped off the boardwalk and gave the horse a critical look. "Fine animal," he said. "Will she make it back?"

"Before midnight."

"You're quite a young man," the colonel said. "Ever think of becoming a soldier? I could use a few like you."

"No sir, I have not. I got to get this message delivered."

Abe vaulted onto Star, spun her and trotted her to the building with the sign that said "PAYMASTER" and dismounted.

Inside, Jonas Kinyon read the directions from Colonel Johnston, then from Porter, and grinned.

"Okay." he said, and ten minutes later folded a piece of paper and put all three documents in a new, large envelope.

"There it is," Kinyon said. "Will you see Porter soon?"

"Tonight."

"Tell that old outlaw if he comes down here, I'll have him arrested and thrown in the stockade for cheating me the last time we played cards."

Abe grinned. "I'll tell him." He walked out the door

and mounted Star, with Kinyon right behind him.

"Better yet," Kinyon said, "tell him he better get on down here so we can play cards again, and this time I'll cheat him."

"Okay. Thanks, Mr. Kinyon."

"No thanks necessary. Be careful. That's a mighty fine horse you got there, and there's lots of people hereabouts that would be right happy to have her."

"I'll be careful. Good luck to you."

Abe tugged the leather loop and Star pivoted and was at her steady run when they passed the soldier with the rifle, at the entry gate.

The sun was reaching for the Oquirrh mountains to the west when Abe stopped to rub and water Star and rest her for five minutes. He remounted and held her at the steady lope until he approached the place where the half dozen men had been camped. He crouched over Star's withers and spoke into her ear, and she leaped to a high run and Abe held the pace for a full minute as he passed the camp, but it was deserted. There was no fire, no camping gear, no men, nothing.

Two hundred yards past the place, he slowed Star to her lope, and two miles later he stopped her and walked her through the brush and willows surrounding Weller's Springs, a small fountain of fresh water that ran eastward to the Jordan River.

He patted her neck while she drank and rested. "Good girl," he said. "A little ways to go, but you'll make it easy."

"Nice horse you got there," came the gruff voice from behind.

Abe spun and faced a man with a battered hat, a scraggly beard stained by tobacco juice, a ragged coat, and a knife in a sheath, tied to his belt.

Abe pivoted to leap onto Star, but from nowhere came

two more grimy men and grabbed the leather loop, while their arms circled Star's neck. Star stuttered her feet and started to fight.

"Better settle that horse, or we'll kill it, and you," the man demanded.

"Be gentle," Abe said to Star, and touched her with the flat of his hand on her neck. She settled and turned to watch him.

"We figgered you'd be coming back, and stop here at the springs. We just want to talk to you for a minute." The man advanced with a wicked smile, and when he was closer he suddenly jerked out his knife and lunged for Abe.

Abe leaped to one side like a cat. Another man rushed toward him and Abe dodged and kicked the man as he floundered past. A third man drew an ancient flintlock pistol and struggled to cock the hammer. Abe ducked and sprinted away from the men, north, dodging through the willows while they cursed and tried to follow. He leaped into the bushes and willows lining the Jordan River, and dodged behind an old tree stump, burned out by a lightning strike years ago.

Three men were struggling with Star, holding her while two others ran to get ropes to tie her.

"Let the boy go," Abe heard the leader cry. "We can sell the horse down south. Let's get moving before he brings the law."

Abe stepped out into full view, and he raised two fingers to his mouth and blew a piercing whistle with all his strength. Then he shouted, "STAR, COME GIRL."

Star reared and the men were thrown back. She struck the man in front of her with her front hooves, and buckled the man behind her with a kick from her back hooves. She roared her defiance and swung her head and bit the hand of the man trying to hold her leather loop. The terrified, injured men fell backwards and threw their hands before their faces to ward off this demon horse, and Star turned her head, searching, and then she saw Abe eighty yards to the north, waiting, and in two jumps she was running full out.

Abe gave her the signal - the one they had practiced until they worked like a perfect team - and Star came past Abe at a run. He took four running steps as she approached, caught the leather loop, and swung onto her back so smoothly she did not have to break stride. He hunched forward and he spoke into her ear, and her head lowered and Star ran as never before.

They heard one single pistol shot that went wild, and then they were out of sight of the gang of cutthroats. Abe held the pace for five full minutes, then slowed Star, then stopped her. Instantly he was off her back, on his knees, checking her feet and ankles and going over her from head to toe while Star stood still.

"Did they hurt you, girl," he said softly, over and over again.

Star was sound. Slowly her heaving sides quieted as she caught her breath.

"Good girl," Abe said as he ripped dry grass in clumps, and wiped her sweated hide. "Good girl. They thought they could take you. You showed them. Good girl."

He led her through the willows to the river, and in a clear sunset, let her drink.

The moon rose as Abe saw the distant lights of Salt Lake City. It was well above the Wasatch mountains when he passed the Redwood Road stagecoach station. It was approaching its zenith when he reined Star eastward on North Temple Street, and then back to the rear wall of the Lion House.

Star sensed a movement in the shadows and shied, and Abe heard a quiet voice, "Be gentle, girl, it's only me."

"Seth! What are you doing here?"

Seth and Hawk slipped out of the shadows.

"We got to know the answer to Porter's letter."

"I got it right here." Abe slipped the large envelope out of his shirt.

Seth whistled once, softly.

The rear gate opened and Porter beckoned them inside. Abe led Star inside the wall.

"You get the answer," Porter asked intently.

Abe handed him the envelope, and Porter thrust it to Seth. "Read it. I'll fetch a lamp."

He returned from the carriage house with a lighted lamp while Seth opened the envelope, and read softly.

Porter:

Myron Brewer was a private in the U. S. Army but was given a dishonorable discharge at Camp Floyd for stealing and attempted murder. He is five feet ten inches tall and weighs 185 pounds and has heavy shoulders and a heavy neck. He is a bad man and will do other mischief. We do not know a man named David McKenzie. Myron Brewer had a friend named Joachim Johnston (no relative of Colonel Johnston who is a good man) and Joachim Johnston drank a lot and was a trouble maker.

I do not have more information. I hope this helps.

Your faithful friend,
Sergeant-Major Jonas Kinyon, U. S. Army.

"The dead man is Joachim Johnston," Seth exclaimed, "and Myron Brewer is the heavy man who killed him."

"Yeah," Porter said, "and that leaves David McKenzie. Myron Brewer wrote to him in St. Louis. Did he come all the way out here to engrave plates for the counterfeiting scheme?"

"I'd bet on it," Seth said.

Porter sighed. "I want to think on this overnight. It's nearly midnight." Suddenly he turned to Abe, as though a thought had struck him. "Say, I forgot to ask. How are you? And how's that horse?"

"I'm fine. Star's tired, but she's fine too."

"Any trouble?"

"Not much."

"What happened."

"Some bad men tried to steal Star."

"Anyone get hurt?"

"Them. They never got her."

"You'll have to tell us the whole story tomorrow. When did you eat last?"

Abe reflected. "Breakfast. Both Star and me."

"Want to come to my diggins? I'll put somethin' on the table."

"No, my mom will be worried and waiting. I told her I was taking Star for a long ride. Star and me do that sometimes."

"I got to tell you, Abe," Porter said, "I been in some tight places where good horseflesh kept me alive, but I never seen a horse that could make that run."

"I know. Star's the best."

They turned towards the gate to leave, Porter leading the way with the lantern.

For a brief moment, Hawk stopped and stared at the ground.

"What's wrong, Hawk," Porter said. "See somethin'?"

Hawk shook his head. "Something caught my eye. Too dark."

Porter held the gate while the boys silently slipped out into the darkness, Abe leading Star.

"I'll be in touch," Porter said. "Stay out of trouble."

They separated, Hawk heading for Temple Square, Abe down East Temple riding Star in the moonlight, and Seth heading east towards State Street.

By one o'clock Hawk was sleeping fitfully. By three o'clock he was sitting quietly in the darkness of his shed, concentrating.

What was it on the ground back there inside the wall. Porter had the lamp, we were leaving, there was a mark on the ground, what was it, why won't it let go.

Suddenly he sat bolt upright.

"Of course," he said out loud. "Of course! How could I forget?"

Nine

SETH STARED AT THE coiled rattler at his feet and felt beads of sweat on his forehead and lip. He dared not move. The cold, beady yellow eyes with the tiny slits in the center fixed him, and the ugly head drew back as the snake coiled.

"He's going to strike, he's going to strike, and I can't move,I can't move," Seth shouted, and then the tail of the snake quivered and the rattling sound grew and crescendoed until it was the only sound in the world.

"I've got to run and my feet won't work–I'm dead–I'm dead," Seth cried.

He wrenched back the covers of his bed and heard his own shouted words bounce off the walls of his dark bedroom. He leaped to the floor and felt the cool, polished hardwood on his bare feet and he looked around and saw the square of faint light coming through his window.

"I . . the snake . . where . ." He felt his face and wiped away the sweat and slumped onto his bed.

"Seth, are you all right," came the voice down the

hallway, and a moment later his mother barged through his door, a lamp in her hand.

"You cried out. Are you all right? What's the matter?"

"Oh mother, am I glad to see you. I had a bad dream. A snake. He was going to strike and I couldn't run."

"Why son," Margaret Dunn said, "you're shaking. Do you want me to warm some milk?"

"No, just let me sit here for a minute while the dream goes away. That's the ugliest snake I ever saw."

"I'll sit with you," Margaret said. "You've been doing too many things, with the newspaper and the youth patrols, and your church work and trying to take care of this place. No wonder you're having bad dreams."

"I'm going down to get a drink of cold water," Seth said, and his mother followed him to the kitchen. He dipped water from the bucket and drank slowly, and glanced at the old wind-up clock on the cupboard. 4:10 in the morning.

"Go on back to bed, mama," he said. "I'll be all right now."

He was back in his bed, eyes wide in the dark, when the rattle came again, and Seth sat bolt upright, eyes darting about, searching in the dark.

It came again, at his window. Slowly he slipped over and raised the blind and peered out.

Two eyes in a dark face peered back at him.

"Hawk!", he whispered hoarsely.

He slipped the window open and thrust his head out. "Hawk, what do you think you're doing?"

"What's all the shouting and the lights about," Hawk said, bewildered.

"You nearly killed me!"

"I did? All I did was rattle the window."

"All you did was give me the fright of my life about rattle snakes."

Hawk's face puckered. "Rattlesnakes? You lost me somewhere in all that."

"I'll explain it later. What brings you here this time of night?"

"I remembered! I saw something when we were with Porter, and I remembered what it was. We got to go back to the Lion House the minute it's light enough."

"Okay okay, but what was it?"

"A footprint."

"Whose?"

"If I'm right, it belongs to Myron Brewer."

Seth's mouth fell open and for long seconds he froze in stunned silence.

"Where?"

"Right there inside the back wall of the Lion House, where Porter has his room."

"Impossible!"

"That's what I think, but I swear, it woke me up. I got to see it in the daylight."

At 5:10 Seth threw grain to the chickens, and started north up the street at a trot, Hawk by his side. They rounded the corner of the back wall of the Lion House at 5:30 and silently scaled it and dropped into the yard.

They waited for a moment; nothing moved.

Hawk carefully retraced his steps of the previous night, bent forward, eyes scouring the ground.

"There," he said excitedly.

"Where," Seth whispered. "I don't see anything."

Hawk dropped to one knee and his finger outlined an impression in he dirt of the path. "Right there. See it?"

"I see a dent."

Hawk studied the ground, then rose and walked, one slow pace at a time, towards the gate.

Suddenly he stopped and again dropped to one knee. "Another one. Yes, those are the same tracks I saw that night at the hotel."

"Brewer was in here?"

"Yes he was."

"When? Can you tell when?" Hawk studied the single

track, then gently touched the edges. "The last three, four days. Not more. And he was carrying something heavy, probably on his right shoulder."

"How do you know?"

"That's a right shoe print, the last one was left. This one is a little deeper."

Seth froze. "Of course! The night of the murder at the Oasis. While we were all there, he brought the body of Joachim Johnston here! No wonder we couldn't find it."

Hawk nodded. "Do you suppose it's still here?"

Seth felt a prickly feeling rise along his spine. "A dead body, here on Brigham Young's property?"

"If Brewer put it here that night, maybe he didn't want to risk moving it. I doubt I would."

Seth swallowed hard, and turned, and whistled softly. Two minutes later a door squeaked open and Porter came out, eyes squinted against the light, pulling a suspender over his shoulder. He wore only his pants, his long handled underwear, and socks.

"Don't you kids ever sleep," he growled.

"You aren't going to believe this," Seth said earnestly, "but Hawk swears Brewer was in this yard about the night of the murder at the Oasis, and he had something heavy over his right shoulder."

Porter fixed a cocked eye on Hawk. "How do you figure that?"

Hawk knelt. "That is a right foot print, still pretty deep, and the same print I read at the Delmonico that night."

He pointed. "Over there's a left print, same man, only not so deep. Nearly gone. He had something heavy over his right shoulder."

Porter dropped to one knee to study the prints. "Well I swan," he muttered. "I woulda missed it, but it looks like you got somethin'. He coulda been here while we was over at the Oasis." He stood and was lost in deep thought for a moment before he suddenly raised a hand. "You suppose that body . . ."

"It might be," Seth said.

"My guess is he wouldn't risk moving it," Hawk said.

Porter's eyes covered everything in the backyard in a few seconds. "Where would he put it? He didn't have but fifteen, twenty minutes."

"Could he have buried it? Did you have any holes dug for trees or shrubs?"

Porter rubbed his whiskered jaw as he tried to remember. "Not that I recall. Let's go look in the carriage house."

For half an hour they moved everything in the carriage house that could hide a body, including the loft where buggy tops were stored.

"Not here," Porter said finally. "I'm goin' in to get a shirt on. You kids look around and I'll be right back."

Five minutes later he joined the boys, searching every tree, behind every bush. Half an hour later he sat down on a tree bench and said, "If he hid it here, he sure hid it good."

Seth looked at the beautiful, carefully pruned and trimmed and weeded rose garden. "Could he have buried it in the rose garden?"

Porter shook his head. "I don't see how. Can't dig a hole in the ground big enough for a man in ten minutes and bury him without everybody seein' the mound."

Hawk slowly turned and faced the northeast corner of the lot.

"No," he said quietly, "but he could scoop a hole in a compost pile and bury a body fast and nobody would notice."

Porter's head swivelled and he slowly stood. None of them spoke as they each picked a hoe or rake from the gardener's tool barrel, and walked to the great pile of grass clippings and tree and flower trimmings heaped in the corner where the two walls met, to decay into rich fertilizer. Dreading the thought, they each slowly pushed the long handles into the compost pile.

Seth's hoe handle struck something solid and stopped. He looked at Porter and pulled the hoe handle out, moved it a foot, and again pushed the handle in. Again it stopped.

Wordlessly Porter fetched a shovel and scooped out great loads of the decaying compost where Seth had worked. On the sixth scoop, Porter gasped and stopped.

A rigid, discolored human hand dangled from the wall of the crater Porter had cleared. Hawk and Seth stood stock still while Porter worked the arm free, then the shoulders and head, and then tugged the body out. He rolled it onto its face and pulled the filthy coat up to expose the back.

Three slits showed in the shirt, surrounded by black, clotted blood.

"Joachim Johnston," Porter said quietly. "This is where Brewer buried him. I would never have guessed."

He paused for a moment, staring at the body, and Seth and Hawk stared at it, in the beauty of a clear, clean, beautiful Wasatch Mountain sunrise. It was as though for that moment they were all unexpectedly seized by a deep, powerful, uninvited feeling of compassion, nearly sadness, for the lifeless form at their feet.

A son of God who lost his way and paid for his sins with his life. He would never again see the breathless beauty of a sunrise, or another sunset, never laugh again, never weep, never know the loving touch of his mother or a wife or a child. In this life, he would never feel his soul quicken as it awakened to the thrilling truths of the gospel, and he would never know the joy of leaving a life of sin, to become a new being, loving and serving his fellow man. He was Joachim Johnston, a son of God who had lost his way, and he now lay lifeless before them.

Porter shuffled his feet and broke the grip of the powerful mood.

"We better take care of him," he said. "Let's clean him up a little and wrap him in a tarp and we'll put him in the carriage house loft for now."

Ten minutes later they walked from the carriage house, back into the sunlight.

Porter hitched up his suspenders. "I think this is the day for the showdown. Today we clean up this mess."

Seth watched Porter's eyes. They narrowed slightly and a glow came into them as they became points of light.

"We got to get David McKenzie, and we got to flush Myron Brewer out in the open and get him too. I doubt McKenzie's a violent man, but Brewer, - well, he'll do anything, kill anybody to save his hide."

He slowly rubbed his stubble beard while he thought.

"We'll start with McKenzie." He glanced at the sun, just clearing the tops of the east mountains. "Right now, before he has a chance to be up and gone."

He looked at the boys. "This is my job. You boys go on about your morning business, but meet me back here in an hour or so."

Porter opened the back gate for them, and turned on his heel and marched to the house without looking back. Fifteen minutes later he returned to the carriage house, clean shaved, in fresh clothes, with a string tie dangling. He hitched a mare to a buggy. Ten minutes later he slowed and stopped in front of Olson's boarding house. He drew a .44 Colt from beneath his coat, checked the loads, holstered it, pulled his low crowned, flat brimmed hat down, and his boots made hollow sounds as he walked onto the porch.

He knocked. Sigrid Olson opened the door and her hand flew to her mouth at recognition of Orrin Porter

Rockwell standing on her front porch in the rose colors of sunrise.

"Good morning," she said when she recovered.

Porter held his hat in his hands. "'Mornin, ma'am. Didn't mean to give you a fright. I need to see John Jones."

"Is there - trouble?"

"No ma'am, I don't expect trouble. But I have to see him."

Sister Olson stepped back and pointed at the stairs. "Upstairs, room eight."

Porter nodded and his boots clumped as ascended the stairs. His steady footsteps made a cadence as he walked to the last room on the left of the long hall.

His knock echoed.

There was no answer.

He knocked again, harder, and listened as sounds of feet hitting the floor came through the door.

"Yeah, who's there?"

Porter remained silent, but knocked once more. Up the hall, a door opened, a head thrust out, then disappeared, and the door closed.

Porter heard the key turn in room eight, and stepped back one step, and his right hand disappeared under his coat. The door opened and David McKenzie stood before him, barefooted, clad only in his hastily buttoned pants. His eyes squinted against the light.

"Who are you," he demanded gruffly. Then his eyes bugged and his head jerked forward and he blurted, "Porter Rockwell!"

He desperately tried to close the door but Porter caught it with his foot and shoved it open and the force threw McKenzie back against his bed. Porter's hand jerked from beneath his coat and McKenzie heard the pistol come to full cock, and then he was staring down the muzzle of a .44 Colt.

Porter closed the door while his blazing eyes fixed McKenzie to the spot.

"Get your clothes on. We're going up town."

McKenzie stammered, "I aint goin'. You aint the law. You got no right, no warrant."

"I'm the law for the Prophet Brigham, and that's law enough. Get washed and dressed or come the way you are."

McKenzie sat down on his bed and put on his socks and shoes, then opened the closet for his shirt. He hung it by the wash stand, then poured water into the basin from the heavy pitcher. McKenzie washed and wiped his face, and did not see Porter move to the closet and take the letter from the old brown coat and slip it into his own inside coat pocket,

McKenzie finished running a comb through his hair, then buttoned on his shirt.

"Where's your black satchel with your tools," Porter demanded.

McKenzie recoiled and blanched. "I aint got it."

Porter lifted the bed covers and peered under the bed. "And the engraving plates?"

McKenzie blurted, "How did you . . . I aint got them neither."

"Where are they?" Porter raised the pistol.

McKenzie jerked up a hand as though to turn away a bullet. "They aint here, I tell you. I moved 'em."

"Where?"

"In town."

"Where in town?"

"In the second floor of Bagley's silversmith shop."

Then he stopped and squared his shoulders and a look of sarcastic defiance crossed his face. "Just like Brigham Young told me."

"Brigham!," Porter spat. "You accusin' Brigham?"

"I'm accusing no one of nothing," McKenzie said. "I'm

only saying what happened."

"We'll see about that. Get downstairs and out to my buggy, and remember, I'm right beside you."

He shoved the pistol back into its shoulder holster and held the door while McKenzie walked out into the hall. Porter shut and locked the door and followed McKenzie downstairs.

"Thank you, Sister Olson," Porter said graciously. "Here's the keys. Mr. Jones will be going with me. Don't wait breakfast on him."

Porter sat like a statue as he drove the buggy back to the Lion house, jaw set, eyes like flint. McKenzie sat beside him, white faced, making small, nervous moves with his hands.

Porter closed the rear gate at the Lion House, unhitched the mare and led her to her stall, and pulled McKenzie inside the carriage house.

"You listen good because I'm goin' to ask you this just once. Where's Myron Brewer?"

"I don't know, I swear I don't know."

Porter drew his pistol. "When did you last see him?"

"I don't remember."

"He helped you move that printing stuff to Bagley's. Where did he go from there?"

"I don't know."

Porter cocked the .44 and levelled it. "Then let's go see the constable. The charge will be first degree murder. You'll hang for that."

"I didn't do no murder," whined McKenzie, squirming.

"Brewer did, and you were in on his scheme, and that makes you guilty right along with him in the eyes of the law. You'll hang on the same gallows."

"You got no proof," cried McKenzie, his voice cracking.

Porter broke a wry smile. "I see Brewer didn't tell

you." He chuckled, then sobered, and thrust his face within eight inches of McKenzies and thundered, "There was two eye witnesses, not five feet away when Brewer threw Johnston out that back door and struck him in the back three times with his knife at the Oasis. And now we got the body to prove it."

"Yeah, you have the body right here on Brigham's property," McKenzie cried. "It looks more like Brigham done it than Brewer."

Porter stepped back one pace. "That was your first mistake, and maybe your last. I didn't tell you the body was here. You knew it because you either helped Brewer bring it here, or he told you about it."

"That's not true," McKenzie shrieked. "You told me, earlier. You told me."

Porter smiled. "Let's go see who the constable believes."

"No no," wailed McKenzie.

"It's over for you, son. You better tell me the whole story. I'll try to keep you from hangin', if you'll tell it all."

The sound of a mourning dove drifted in through the open door. Porter took a rope from a wall peg and tied McKenzie's hands to the spokes of a carriage wheel. "You stay here."

He holstered his pistol and walked out into the morning sun and closed the door. He raised his hands to his lips to signal Seth not to speak, and he led them over to the rose garden.

"McKenzie's inside. We got to talk low so he doesn't find out you two are in this," Porter said quietly. "He's about to tell me his story."

"Did you get his tools and the printing equipment," Seth asked.

"No, he and Brewer moved them to Bagley's

silversmith shop sometime last night. I don't know why, yet."

"Where's Brewer?," Seth asked. "I don't know but I think he does. I'll know before long." He pulled the brown letter taken from McKenzie's coat, from his inside pocket and thrust it at Seth.

"Read that."

Seth quickly read the two page letter, then raised wide eyes to Brigham. "That's the answer!"

"Yep," Porter said, "Brewer came close to gettin' it done, too."

Seth thought for a moment. "Would it be smart to get McKenzie's story in writing, so Brewer won't be able to kill him too, and lie out of it?"

"Yeah," Porter said embarrassed, "but I can't read. I wouldn't know if he done it right."

Hawk interrupted. "McKenzie doesn't know that."

Porter squinted an eye at Hawk. "I'll get some paper and a pencil."

Three minutes later Porter returned from his room. "Stay around. I don't know how long this will take, but when it's over, I'm going after Brewer, and I might need you. He's moved around enough. Today's the day we stop him."

Porter let them out through the gate, closed it behind them, and turned back to the door into the carriage shed. Inside, he laid pencil and paper on a barrel top and untied McKenzie.

"Start from the beginning. I'll be reading it while you write. You get one thing wrong, and I'll see you hang."

Seth stopped Hawk beneath the great wooden Eagle.

"Porter says he might need us. You go get the rest of the Brigade, fast. And tell Jacob to bring his rifle. No telling what will happen when we try to corner Brewer."

Ten

THERE WERE THOSE IN Salt Lake City who had seen it before. When Orrin Porter Rockwell walked out into those broad, dusty streets with his coat off, his black hat low and level, both pistols belted around his lean middle and a third one tucked under his arm in a shoulder holster, and his spurs jingling, those were the people who quietly vanished from the streets, and peered from behind window curtains, or around corners, to watch.

Such was the occurrence just before noon on this clear, hot summer's day. With measured, steady stride, Porter walked down the middle of State Street, past the bank building, across First South, on past ZCMI, to the middle of the block. He walked directly to the side of the two storied, wooden building with the BAGLEY'S SILVERSMITH sign opposite ZCMI, and stopped at the foot of the outside stairs leading to the second floor - the only way up or down.

He drew each pistol in turn, checked the loads, flexed

the hammer, and settled them back into their holsters. His boots thumped on each of the fourteen steps leading to the second floor. He turned the door handle and pushed the door inward, and flattened himself against the outside wall for five seconds.

Nothing moved, and there was no sound.

He darted through the doorway and flattened himself against the inside wall while he waited for his eyes to adjust to the dim light before he started down the hallway. He opened the first door on his right and waited, but there was no sound. He walked to the second door and threw it open.

Nothing.

He continued to the third.

Down in the street, Libby darted through the gathering crowd and came up beside Seth.

"He's up there," Seth said and pointed, "after Brewer."

Libby's breathing quickened.

The sound of hooves brought both their heads around as Abe leaped from Star's back half a block away and came dodging through the crowd.

"Up there," Libby said, and pointed.

Jacob came up behind them, face tipped upward, spellbound as he watched the vacant stairway.

Hawk appeared from nowhere, beside Jacob.

Inside, Porter turned the handle of the last door on the right side of the hallway and pushed it open.

Again, silence.

From behind him, on the left, came the sound of a handle being turned slowly, carefully, and then the sound of a door being thrown wide open and footsteps pounding in the hallway. Porter threw himself across the hall against the wall as he spun and drew both pistols. He felt the tug of a bullet on his shirt sleeve and heard the roaring blast of a pistol at the same instant and he saw the shape of a heavy shouldered man dodge through the doorway to outside and Porter fired both pistols at once and knew one bullet had hit. The other had splintered the door jamb as the man disappeared, and Porter heard the heavy pounding of boots on the stairs.

The crowd in the streets gasped and shrank back at the sound of the blasting pistols, and women shrieked and men shouted when Myron Brewer came thundering down the stairs waving a revolver. Brewer broke from the side of the building and ran to the center of the street and spun around to face the building, pistol raised, waiting for Porter to appear on the staircase.

Jacob held his breath for a moment, then grabbed Hawk.

"Come on," he snapped. He spun and sprinted, Hawk right behind. In a moment he was behind ZCMI where his horse was tied. He jerked his Henry repeater rifle from the scabbard and slipped the sling over his shoulder. He ran to the fire escape and scrambled to the top of the building, Hawk following.

The front of ZCMI was a facade that rose four feet above roof level, and both Jacob and Hawk peered over. Brewer stood in the street eighty feet away, facing Bagley's store, his pistol cocked and aimed up the staircase.

Jacob gauged the distance and settled the Henry against his shoulder, the barrel cradled in his left hand, his left arm steadied on the facade. He jacked the lever down and watched the fat, stubby, yellow brass cartridge lift into position, and the closing bolt drove it into the firing chamber.

He levelled the rifle and waited.

Porter glanced at the dirty tear in his shirt sleeve. There was no blood.

He waited a moment, re-cocked both pistols, then darted out onto the second floor landing, pistols thrust out in front, and turned to face the street. ready. Brewer fired and his bullet smacked through the open door behind Porter, not two inches from his head. Porter fired both pistols at once and his bullets blasted dirt on both sides of Brewer.

"Surrender," Porter shouted, "or the next two kill you. You won't get another chance."

Brewer ran to his left, out of Porter's sight, while Porter leaped down the staircase, and as Porter burst into the street, Brewer suddenly veered toward the shocked, stunned crowd.

"Look out," Seth screamed as Brewer closed on him and Libby, and he shoved Libby roughly one way and Seth dove the other. Brewer scooped Libby from the ground and spun and ran back to the middle of the street to face Porter with his pistol pressed against Libby's back.

"Throw down your guns, Rockwell," Brewer demanded, "or I kill the Mayor's daughter." A wicked, hysterical laugh came rolling from his throat. "You're going to get me a buggy, and then I'm leaving town, and I'm taking the girl. Anybody follows me, you'll find her remains out there in the desert for the wolves and coyotes."

Porter turned sideways to Brewer and held his right pistol with the muzzle up, waiting for a clear shot.

"Porter!" He heard the familiar voice softly, to one side and he glanced quickly.

In that moment Seth turned his face upward to the ZCMI facade, and Porter's eyes followed. He saw the muzzle of the Henry, and Jacob's head with Hawk's next to it.

Slowly Porter began to walk to his left, making a great circle around Brewer in the street, and Brewer turned as he walked, always keeping Libby between himself and Porter's pistol. The red blotch was growing on Brewer's left shoulder where Porter's bullet had struck.

"You heard me," Brewer bawled. "Throw down your guns."

"Can't do that," Porter said. "You're finished. You got a bullet in your shoulder. Someone's going to have to dig it out and do some doctorin' or you'll die. You won't go far."

Brewer thrust his right arm straight out and aimed his pistol at Porter's chest.

Porter continued his circling walk. Just a little further. Just a little further. Got to get him sideways to Jacob. Sideways. Just a little further.

Brewer's face suddenly wrenched into an ugly mask. "Drop it now, or I kill you," he said.

Jacob watched, tense, waiting. A little further, just enough to get that pistol sideways to me so I got a good angle, keep walking, keep it up. There!

He took a breath and released it, took another and released half of it, then lined the thin blade of the foresight in the center of the notch of the rear sight, then onto the pistol hand of Brewer, and he fired three shots as fast as he could lever the rifle.

The first shot blasted the pistol from Brewer's hand, the second ripped his hat from his head and knocked it rolling in the dust, and the third smashed the bone handle of his sheathed knife on his near hip. The force of the third bullet strike knocked Brewer staggering sideways, shocked, stunned, and he tried to catch his balance and he lost his hold on Libby. She kicked and wrenched free and ran to Seth and Abe, and collapsed against them sobbing.

Brewer went down on one knee and Porter was on top of him before he could recover his balance. Porter jammed the muzzle of his cocked pistol under Brewer's jaw and he rasped out through gritted teeth, "Make a move. Any move. I'm beggin'."

Brewer looked into Porter's eyes, and he saw lightning from the eternal pit, and all the fight went out of him.

Porter called, "Get Constable Hastings," and a man

with a badge pushed through the crowd.

"Take him. Charge him with murder and counterfeiting."

"No such thing," Brewer shouted.

"I got the body," Porter exclaimed, "and that aint all. I got David McKenzie and he wrote out the whole story and signed it. I got it right here."

"It was Brigham Young put us up to it," Brewer shouted, and everyone in the street suddenly fell silent.

He took heart from the sudden change of mood in the crowd. "That's right! Brigham Young. You let me and McKenzie go, we'll tell you the whole story. It was Brigham Young made us do it, and it was him that hid the body. Why, Porter Rockwell did a crime, shooting me like he done. I only shot back in self defense."

The constable paused and looked at Porter. "Is there any truth to this?" A murmur arose in the crowd.

Porter held up his hands for silence. He drew two envelopes from his pants pocket and raised one of them.

"This is a signed confession by David McKenzie. He was the engraver hired by this man to make the counterfeit money you all know about. McKenzie wrote out the whole story. Brewer is the man who is responsible, and who killed another man named Joachim Johnston."

"He lied," Brewer shouted. "If McKenzie said that, he lied."

Porter held up the second envelope. "Brewer can call McKenzie's confession a lie, but in this envelope is a letter that he can not call a lie."

The crowd silenced.

"This letter was written by Brewer himself to David McKenzie in St. Louis. In this letter, Brewer lays out the whole scheme, start to finish, including a way to blame it all on Brigham Young. Brewer and his friend Joachim Johnston were going to finish the counterfeiting and then put the plates in a room above Bagley's, because Brigham

Young owns that building. They were going to claim Brigham did all the counterfeiting to get even with the army for coming here and setting up Camp Floyd. You'll find the counterfeit plates and McKenzies engraving tools up there in one of those rooms above Bagley's, and I don't think any of you will forget that I had to go flush Brewer out of there, where he hid them."

He lowered his hand and the envelope.

"And you'll find the dead body of Joachim Johnston down at the Lion House where Brewer put it after he killed Johnston because Johnston got drunk and talked too much at the Oasis. You'll find McKenzie down there too, tied up in the carriage barn."

He thrust both envelopes into the hands of the constable. "Don't lose 'em. They will convict this murderer."

Hastings locked handcuffs on Brewer and the angry crowd followed them off towards the jail.

Jacob turned and ran for the back of the building. "We got to get down from here before anyone sees us," he said. "No one is supposed to find out we were mixed up in this. Get on down quick and catch my rifle."

Hawk was on the ground in five seconds and Jacob carefully lofted his Henry outward and Hawk caught it out of the air and quickly slid it back into its scabbard while Jacob scrambled down the fire escape.

The crowd suddenly remembered the unbelievable shooting that had stopped Brewer without harming him, and raised their faces to the ZCMI facade.

"Who was that up there?"

"That had to be an army marksman."

"There isn't anyone in the army can shoot like that."

"Do you suppose that was Jacob Pierce? Him and that repeater rifle of his?"

"I don't know. I didn't see. He can shoot like that, though." Three minutes later Jacob and Hawk were mingling in the crowd, looking upward, pointing, exclaiming, "Who was that up there? Why, that shooting was impossible."

Ladies suddenly descended on Libby.

"You poor, brave dear!"

"That awful man - he must have given you such a fright."

Libby had partially recovered from the shock of having a murderer thrust his pistol into her back and threaten to kill her while he hauled her into the middle of the street. She put on her most humble, fetching smile.

"Oh it was nothing, really."

"Child, that man is a murderer!"

"I know, but really, it was nothing."

"Here, let me help you home."

"Oh thank you ever so much, but I'm sure my father will be here shortly. Please don't worry about me. It was a little - frightening - but it will pass."

She pressed the back of her hand to her forehead and grasped Seth's sleeve to steady herself.

Jacob looked at her and rolled his eyes into his head, and started for the back of ZCMI to his horse and rifle, shaking his head.

Hawk grinned.

Abe headed back to Star.

Seth held her up.

Libby gazed up at him and said, "Isn't he wonderful?"

"Who?"

"Jacob."

"He certainly is. He saved you and stopped Brewer."

"I know."

"Oh Jacob," Libby called. "Just a moment." She walked swiftly to his side and gently laid her hand on his arm. "Thank you. You saved my life."

Jacob looked into her eyes and felt the familiar tightening in his chest. "It wasn't much. You're welcome."

"What wasn't much?" she asked in feigned disappointment.

"My life?"

"Aw, Libby," he said, "come on. You know better than that. The shooting. It wasn't much."

"No one else could have done it."

Jacob looked at her hopefully. "I'm glad you're okay. Really glad."

Libby saw the shine in Jacob's eyes, and suddenly she smiled her charming smile. "Isn't he wonderful?"

The air went out of Jacob and his shoulders sagged. "Yeah. I know. He's just wonderful."

* * *

"Yer to come with me."

Seth flinched at the sudden sound from the shadows of the milk barn, then relaxed instantly at recognition of the twangy voice.

He grinned as the shadowy shape walked into the lantern light. "Porter, how are you?"

"Good. Brigham wants to see you."

They walked side by side in the softness of the warm night air, past the pen where Mossie worked on her cud, on up Second East by the big irrigation canal. At the aspen trees, Seth waited with Porter while the blocky shape emerged and walked to them.

The Prophet thrust out his hand. "How are you tonight, Brother Dunn?"

"I'm fine, sir," Seth replied, and they shook hands warmly, as two old friends.

"Porter told me about it. You saved me. I will be eternally in debt to you and your friends."

Brigham turned towards the temple, shining in the moonlight.

"The work of the Lord will roll on and no hand will stop it, but we must be vigilant always. We must be gentle as doves and clever as foxes."

Seth could see the smile in the strong square face. "Porter calls you Brigham's Ghost Brigade. I like that." He paced a few feet and then returned, head bowed in deep thought. "Seth," he said after a few moments, "I've had some hard things told me in the past few days. The transcontinental railroad is nearly finished. One of the greatest historical events in the history of this country, one that will bring men from high positions in our government to the celebration."

He raised his face directly to Seth's.

"I've been told there is a plot to blow up the parts of the railroad and kidnap those important men, and either kill them or hold them for ransom."

He paused for a moment.

"I think finding out about such a plot is a job for you and your friends."

Seth caught his breath.

"What do you say?," the Prophet asked quietly.

"I say yes, sir. If you want us to do it, we will."

Brigham turned to Porter, standing quietly beside them in the soft moonlight.

"What do you say?"

"Brigham's Ghost Brigade?," Porter answered. "Old wheat in the mill."